THE LEGEND LIVES

"On my word you will throw your weapons down."

Bold Wolf turned his head and saw Clint Adams standing just above him, holding a gun.

The other braves were looking at Clint, too, and behind him at Many Horses, holding a rifle.

"Many Horses, shoot this white man," Bold Wolf said.

Clint was relieved to hear Many Horses. say, "I cannot, Bold Wolf."

"We can kill him easily," Bold Wolf told the others. "We are six to one. Many Horses will not shoot him, but he will not shoot us, either." Bold Wolf looked at Clint with disdain and said, "He is not the Dreamwalker."

"I don't have to be," the Gunsmith said, cocking the hammer of the gun and pointing it directly at Bold Wolf's head, "to kill you . . . "

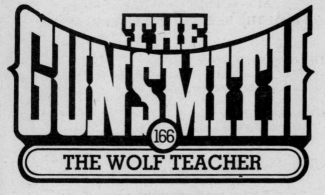

THE GUNSMITH

166

THE WOLF TEACHER

J. R. ROBERTS

JOVE BOOKS, NEW YORK

THE WOLF TEACHER

A Jove Book / published by arrangement with
the author

PRINTING HISTORY
Jove edition / October 1995

ISBN: 0-515-11732-3

A JOVE BOOK®
Jove Books are published by The Berkley Publishing Group,
200 Madison Avenue, New York, New York 10016.
JOVE and the "J" design are trademarks
belonging to Jove Publications, Inc.

PRINTED IN THE UNITED STATES OF AMERICA

10 9 8 7 6 5 4 3 2 1

THE GUNSMITH

166

THE WOLF TEACHER

ONE

It was as strange an occurrence as Clint Adams had ever run across. If he didn't know better he would have sworn that the animal had come out of nowhere. In fact, it was odd that his big, black gelding, Duke, had not been able to sniff the animal out long before it got to within striking distance.

Clint had camped for the night and had a pot of coffee on the fire, along with a pan of bacon. He was two days out of Denver, where he'd spent some time visiting his friend Bat Masterson.

He finished his dinner and poured himself another cup of coffee. Momentarily leaving it on the ground, he walked over to where Duke was standing just to check on him. The horse had taken a bad step during the day and while it hadn't seemed serious at the time Clint wanted to check the leg for swelling.

That's when it happened.

Seemingly from nowhere the bear came from out of the darkness. It moved swiftly and silently. It took one swipe at Clint with a massive paw. The animal's claws went through his shirt and tore three long rents in his back. Clint staggered and went down, clawing for his gun.

The bear then went for Duke, but the horse reared back and lashed out with his front hooves. Clint didn't see what happened, but as suddenly as it had appeared, the bear was gone.

At least, he thought it was a bear.

Gun in hand but still on the ground, Clint looked around him, waiting to see if the animal would strike again. His back was burning, and he could feel the blood there. He didn't know how badly he was hurt, but he knew he had to do something to stop the bleeding.

He got unsteadily to his feet and took a quick look at Duke. While the animal's eyes were wide and his nostrils were flaring, he did not seem to be injured. That was good. No matter how bad Clint's wounds were, he did not like the odds of surviving out here on foot. At least he'd be able to ride out in the morning.

Still holding his gun he moved to the fire, hoping that if the bear had ideas of attacking again the fire would dissuade it. Duke was not tied, so he'd be free to flee or fight, whichever it came to. The big gelding was going to have to watch out for himself. Clint had to do something about the blood he was losing.

He removed his shirt and looked at the back. There were three long tears, and it was soaked with his blood. He set a blanket out on the ground, laid the shirt out on it, and then lay down on his back. He hoped that by staying that way for a while the bleeding would slow or stop. If that happened he could put on a clean shirt, maybe keeping the old one on his back as a makeshift bandage. He tried tying it around him, using the sleeves and the tail, but it wasn't very effective. Instead he just had to lie there and even being by the fire and holding his gun did not stop him from feeling very vulnerable. . . .

He woke up with a start, surprised and dismayed that he had fallen asleep. The bear could have come into camp and taken his head off. He tried to move but it caused so much pain in his back that he stopped. He felt stiff, and his back felt sticky. The shirt, which was supposed to act like a bandage, was plastered to his back with dried blood. He was afraid that moving now would start him bleeding again, but he didn't have much of a choice. He couldn't just lie there. For one thing, he wasn't sure that he wouldn't fall asleep again. His skin felt hot and there was heat behind his eyes. He knew he was feverish and he knew there was a risk of infection. If there had been a water hole or a stream nearby he could have simply waded in and allowed it to wash his back, but he was at least a day's ride from the nearest water.

He stared at the stars in the sky, trying to muster the strength to sit up, but before he could do that he passed out again. . . .

"Well?" Tucker Spring asked.

"One man at a camp fire," Earl Bunch said.

"You sure he's alone?" Ben Fall asked.

"Alone and on the ground."

"Sleeping?"

"I don't think so," Bunch said. "I think he's hurt."

Tucker Spring gave that some thought. He was in his late thirties, a tall man who would have been handsome were it not for a nose that was twice the size it should have been.

Bunch and Fall were in their late twenties, and deferred in most matters to the older man. Bunch was short, about five six, with a temper that was born from the teasing he took as a child and a teenager for his lack of height. He had run away from home at seventeen, when he killed a bigger boy with his hands for teasing him in front of a girl.

Ben Fall was tall and rangy with a sharp nose and hardly any chin. He had no will of his own to speak of and had always been easily led by others, which was how he had become an outlaw in the first place.

"Whataya think, Tuck?" Fall asked.

"I say let's go in and take a look," Spring said. "If he is down and hurt we shouldn't have any trouble with him at all."

He looked at Bunch and asked, "What's it look like he's got?"

"Couldn't tell from where I was, but I know one thing. He's got a helluva horse."

"Horse and rig and whatever he's got in his saddlebags and pockets," Spring said. "Well, the only way to find out is to go and take a look. Come on. . . . "

TWO

The next time he woke up three men were looking down at him.

"Looks like you got messed up pretty bad," one of them said.

"Grizzly . . ." was all he could manage.

"Grizzly bear, here?" one of the others said, looking around.

The sky above them was starting to get light.

"I could use some help," Clint said.

The three men continued to stare at him. They seemed to range in age from early twenties to mid-thirties, and the older one was heavier. All he noticed about the other two was that one was short and the other didn't seem to have a chin.

The older one crouched down next to Clint and then rolled him over just a bit to take a look. Clint winced at the pain.

"Whooee, you been cut up pretty bad. Looks like some infection there, too." He released Clint and let him roll onto his back again. "Don't look like you're gonna last too long, mister."

"Need help . . ."

The man stood up.

"Ben, see what you can find around here that's worth taking."

"Right, Tuck."

"Earl, get the horse."

"Right, Tuck."

The one called Ben crouched over Clint and started going through his pockets.

"You—you're robbing me?"

"Looks like it."

"W-why? You could help me."

"I'm afraid I'm more concerned with helping myself, friend. Sorry. Besides, this is just like robbing a dead man."

"Hey, wait—" Clint said, reaching weakly for the man, who batted his arm away easily.

"Just relax, friend, let it come. We all got to go sometime."

Clint's vision was blurring. He heard a commotion, the sound of Duke whinnying and of a man shouting.

"What the hell—" the man called Ben shouted, but as he stood up Clint spiraled down a long dark hole. . . .

He remembered waking many times after that. At least, he thought he was awake. Once there seemed to be just the sun, a big orange ball that filled the sky and burned into his eyes.

Another time there was smoke, a lot of smoke, and he squinted to try to see through it, but couldn't. Also, with the smoke came heat and he felt himself melting . . . no, not melting, but sweating . . .

Later, he saw a face, a beautiful face hovering over him, still partially obscured in smoke. He heard something, too, something that sounded like singing . . . or chanting . . .

Later still a vision of a wrinkled face, the face of an old man, an ancient man, hovering above him, bending down over him and studying him, then touching him . . .

There were dreams, too . . . or maybe they were all dreams . . .

Dreams of a black stallion that could or could not have been Duke . . .

Dreams of a wolf, watching him . . . of a bear, chasing him . . . of an eagle, only he was the watcher . . . and dreams of a snake, coiled and ready to strike, but not striking . . .

It was difficult to separate dream from vision, dream from reality, vision from reality, and sometimes the easiest thing for him to do was just close his eyes and sleep. . . .

When they were far enough away from Clint's camp, the three men stopped to see what they had made off with. By the early light of morning they went through the saddlebags and came up with a clean shirt, a small gun neither had ever seen the likes of before, and about ten dollars. There were also a couple of decks of cards.

"That's it?" Spring said in disgust.

"If we coulda got that horse—" Bunch started, but Ben Fall cut him off.

"Well, we didn't and it wasn't my fault. I couldn't even get near it—and if I did, it probably woulda killed me."

"Forget it, forget it," Spring said, tossing the clean shirt on the ground. He looked at the small gun again, then tucked it into his belt.

"We'll sell the saddle along with the saddlebags and rifle. We should get somethin' for that."

"What about that belly gun?" Fall asked.

Spring looked down at it.

"I might just keep it for myself," he said, looking back at his two partners. "Any objections?"

"No," Bunch said, exchanging a look with Fall, "I ain't got any. You, Ben?"

"Would it do any good?" Fall asked.

"No," Tucker Spring told him, "no good at all."

"You know," Bunch said, "I kinda feel sorry for the guy."

"What?" Fall asked.

"Well, lyin' there all slashed up and all and then we come along and rob him."

"What do you think he woulda done to you if he found you like that?" Fall asked.

Bunch shrugged.

"Well, I don't know. Maybe he woulda helped me."

"Earl, you're too stupid to believe," Fall said. "He woulda done the same thing to you that we done to him. Nobody is gonna help you in this world. You gotta help yourself."

Bunch looked at Spring, who said, "He's right, Earl. You got a sentimental streak in you that you got to get rid of, boy."

"I guess . . ." Bunch said.

"Let's get movin'," Spring said. "I want to put a little more distance between us and that fella's camp before *we* camp."

THREE

He finally woke for good.

The last time he actually remembered being awake he had been able to look up at the night sky. He was lying on his side now, but as he looked up above him he saw that there was no sky, night or otherwise. He was inside, but he wasn't in a house, he was in what appeared to be a tipi.

He remained on his side and took stock of his condition. He frowned, trying to remember what had happened, and then he saw the bear in his mind's eye and flinched instinctively. He remembered. The bear had come out of nowhere, huge, standing on its hind legs, and had swiped at him with a massive paw. Claws had raked his back. The animal went after Duke, but the big gelding fought back, and the bear then disappeared as quickly and quietly as it had appeared.

He'd been injured, he knew that. He had tried to treat himself but he remembered feeling feverish. He must have passed out and then . . . what? How had he come to be here? And where was here?

He looked at his surroundings now and saw the sides of the

tent he was in, covered with drawings that he had thought were dreams. Animals . . . a bear, an eagle, a wolf, a snake, and a horse, among others. He had been inside Indian tipis before, but none like this. It appeared to be a shaman's tent.

The flap of the tipi was thrown back suddenly and he saw a woman enter. She stopped short when she saw that he was awake, then smiled and came toward him. She knelt next to him and touched his forehead.

"You are warm," she said, "but not hot."

She was right, of course. He no longer felt the heat behind his eyes.

"How do you feel?"

He tried to answer, but no words came out. She turned away, and when she turned back she held a wooden ladle with water in it. She held it so he could sip it, wetting his lips and tongue.

"I feel . . . better," he said.

She smiled.

"That is good."

He studied her face, which was dark and beautiful. It was the face he had seen in a dream, or a vision, or so he thought. He was pleased to find out that she was real.

"My horse . . ."

"The mighty one is safe."

"The . . . mighty one?"

"The sacred Black Stallion. Where did you find him?"

He frowned.

"I didn't find him," he said. "I was riding him."

"How long has he been with you?"

He closed his eyes and said, "I don't know . . . forever it seems like. How did I get here?"

"We brought you. Some of our braves found you. You were unconscious. . . . "

"I was robbed," he said, remembering suddenly.

"Not by my people."

"No," he said, "by mine. Three men. They went through my pockets, went for my horse . . . what did they take?"

"Everything."

"But not my horse."

"The mighty stallion was not there when my people found you, but he followed the braves back here. He would not leave you. That's when we knew."

"Knew what?"

"That you were the Dreamwalker."

"The . . . what?"

"The Dreamwalker, he who talks to the Horse and rides the great stallion."

"I don't understand . . ."

Suddenly, he was very tired.

"You must sleep," she said, putting her hand on his head.

"I don't want to sleep. . . . "

"Sleep is good. This will be a healing sleep, not a fevered sleep. It will be good."

"Good . . ." he said.

FOUR

When he woke up again he felt infinitely better. He actually sat up. He noticed for the first time that he was naked to the waist. His boots were also gone, but he was still wearing his pants. Naturally, his gun was gone, as well.

There was some pulling on his back, but he was able to make it without bleeding again. He was sitting there, wondering if he should try to stand when the girl entered again.

"Hello," he said.

"You are sitting up."

"Yes."

"You should not be."

"I feel better."

"I know," she said, kneeling next to him, "but you should not rush. You have much healing to do. Let me look."

She got behind him to look at his back.

"How does it look?" he asked.

"You will have scars."

"That's all right," he said. "It could have been a lot worse."

13

He felt her feather light touch on his back, tracing the wounds.

"You are healing quickly."

"Thanks to you."

She came around in front of him again.

"Not me, my father."

"Is your father a shaman?"

"Yes."

He studied her for a moment and said, "You are Comanche?"

"Yes."

He nodded.

"I am very grateful to you and your father. When will I meet him?"

"He will come and see you later today."

"He was here, wasn't he, when I was unconscious?"

"Oh yes," she said, "he sat with you the first few nights, all night."

"And you," he said, "I remember seeing you . . ."

"I was here also," she said, looking down humbly. She looked at him again then and said, "But it was my father who saved you."

"I must repay you both," he said.

She gave him a grim look and said, "You will."

"What do you—"

"I must go now," she said, standing up. "I will bring you some food."

"Good," he said, "I'm just now feeling hungry."

"You will not stand up."

He looked back at her and said, "I will not stand up."

"Promise."

"I promise."

He kept his promise. He remained seated, but while he was he stretched his arms and legs, testing them. When he stretched his arms too far reaching for water it put a strain on the wounds on his back. He wondered how bad they were. He knew that they had grown infected, but he still didn't know how badly he'd been clawed. It *felt* like he'd been ripped open, but it was hard to judge a wound on your own back.

Just by coincidence when the girl returned he was sitting just as he had been when she left. She carried a wooden bowl with her.

"I have brought you something to eat."

He'd had nothing since she left except water, and he was famished.

She sat next to him and held a piece of meat to his mouth. He knew better than to ask what it was. Indians generally ate whatever they could find. It was not uncommon for them to eat snake, dog, or even a mule or a horse.

He chewed the first piece, then reached for the bowl and said, "I can do it."

"I am nursing you," she said. "You will let me feed you."

"All right." He was hungry and it was better than arguing with her. Besides, he had the feeling he wasn't going to win very many arguments with her.

"You haven't told me your name," he said between bites.

"Tenawa."

"That's a beautiful name. Where does it come from?"

"It was an old tribe of the People that is now dead. I am honored to carry the name."

Clint knew that it had been the whites who had named the Indians Comanche, or Cheyenne, or Sioux and such. They called themselves simply "the People."

"You are far from the reservation," Clint said.

"We cannot live on the reservation," she said simply. Clint did not question her. He knew what kind of conditions the once proud Comanches were living under. After battling the Texans for forty years the Comanches were finally defeated by Colonel Ranald Mackenzie and the Fourth Cavalry. Clint had known Mackenzie and did not like him. He had also known the Comanche war chief Quanah Parker, and had great respect for the man.

She finished feeding him and gave him some water.

"There," she said. "With a full belly you will heal faster."

"Thank you, Tenawa."

She started to get to her feet, but he stopped her by taking hold of her wrist.

"Don't you want to know my name?"

"You are the Dreamwalker."

"I am Clint Adams," he said.

"Clint?"

"Yes."

"That is what you wish to be called?"

"It is."

She nodded.

"Then I shall call you Clint."

"Thank you. When will your father be here?"

"Soon."

"And what is his name?"

"He is Standing Stone."

"It's a strong name."

"He is a strong man," she said proudly. "He is old now, but still strong."

"I look forward to meeting him and thanking him for saving my life."

She nodded and stood up. This time he did not try to stop her.

"When will you come back?"

"After my father leaves," she said, "I will come back to see if you need me."

"Thank you, Tenawa."

She looked away shyly when he said her name.

"Will you do me a favor?" he asked.

"Yes."

"Will you see if my horse is all right?"

"The Black Stallion is a sacred animal." She frowned, perhaps wondering why such an animal would need care.

"It's all right," Clint said. "You can approach him. He likes pretty girls."

"Then I will see to him."

"Make sure he's fed, please?"

"As if he were not a sacred animal?"

Poor ol' Duke, Clint thought. The Comanches were so convinced he was sacred that they probably didn't think he needed to eat.

"Yes," he said. "The Black Stallion loves to eat."

"I will see to it right away."

"Thank you."

She nodded, backing toward the tent flap, and then hurried through it. It hadn't occurred to him before that she might be frightened of him, thinking that he was this Dreamwalker. He was going to have to find out all he could about this legend.

FIVE

The next time the flap of the tipi was thrown open, a man stepped in. He was tall and thick around the middle, but Clint could easily see where once he had been tall and powerfully built. He still had a broad chest and wide shoulders, and even though there was thickness around his middle it was not soft. He was almost completely covered by a blanket, with only one shoulder showing.

His face was a mass of lines and wrinkles. He was Tenawa's father, and she appeared to be in her early twenties. This man could have been anything from fifty to eighty.

"Standing Stone?" Clint asked.

The man nodded.

"I must give you my gratitude for saving my life," Clint said.

"You brought us the Black Stallion," Standing Stone said.

Clint hoped that wasn't meant the way it sounded. He would hate to think that when he left they wouldn't let him take Duke with him.

"You spoke of the bear," Standing Stone said, "and he left his mark on your back."

"Yes, he sure did."

"Do you speak to the Black Stallion?"

"Yes, I do."

"And to the bear?"

"No, I did not speak to the bear."

"Did the bear speak to you?"

"He did not."

"And the Black Stallion? He speaks to you?"

Well, in a way . . . actually, he and Duke did have their own method of communication.

"Yes, he does."

"Then you are the Dreamwalker."

"If I am the Dreamwalker," Clint said, choosing his words carefully, "then I do not remember it. Perhaps my wound, at the claws of the bear, has robbed me of my memory."

Standing Stone seemed to consider that.

"Is it possible?"

"It is possible," the Indian admitted.

"Then perhaps you could tell me of this Dreamwalker," Clint suggested. "If you do this, perhaps it will bring my memory back."

Standing Stone pointed at Clint.

"If you are not the Dreamwalker, then you have deceived us."

"It was not my intention—"

"There are those in camp who did not want to help you," he said.

"Well, I'm glad you didn't listen to them."

"There are those in camp," Standing Stone went on, "who would kill you if they thought you had deceived us."

"Like I said," Clint replied, "it was not my intention to deceive you. Perhaps when I have fully recovered from my wounds—"

"We will speak of this again," Standing Stone said. "I will send my daughter in to tend to you."

"Standing Stone—"

The Comanche shaman held his hand up for silence.

"I will send my daughter in," he said. "We will speak tomorrow."

"All right," Clint said. "Until tomorrow."

Standing Stone nodded, then bent and went out. Moments later Tenawa came in.

"How do you feel?"

"Confused."

"Do your wounds hurt?"

"No."

"Let me look at them."

She came around and knelt down behind him to examine his wounds. She touched them lightly, making them tingle, but they didn't hurt.

"How long have I been here, Tenawa?" he asked.

"Six days and nights."

The wounds on his back would hardly have healed at all in that time.

"Why am I not bandaged?"

"Your wounds do not require bandages."

"My wounds were bad, were they not? Deep? Infected?"

"In-fected?" She was unfamiliar with the word.

"Filled with poison."

"Oh, yes. My father made the poison go away."

"And have the wounds healed?"

"They have not, but they will soon."

He was amazed. He would have expected wounds like he must have had to take a long time to heal. Whatever Standing Stone had done must have worked like . . . magic.

"Is it true?" she asked.

"Is what true?"

"That you do not remember being the Dreamwalker?"

"It is true."

"How can that be? You are the Dreamwalker. You are sacred."

He did some quick thinking.

"The Bear is a sacred animal, is he not?"

"Yes."

"Couldn't a sacred animal injure a sacred man?"

"It . . . is possible."

"I'm sure my memory will come back soon, Tenawa."

"I am worried."

"About what?"

"There are men in camp who would do you harm, kill you . . . if you are not the Dreamwalker."

"Will they wait to find out?"

"They will not go against my father unless they are sure."

"Then they will wait," Clint said, "and so will we."

"I hope," she said sincerely, "that we do not have to wait too long."

SIX

Alone in the tipi Clint realized his predicament. Although the Indians—specifically Standing Stone and his daughter Tenawa—had saved his life, his life was now in danger. It was probably Duke who had saved his life in the first place. When the Comanches found him and saw Duke they must have figured that if Duke was the Black Stallion, then he must be the Dreamwalker. Now, if it turned out that he was not the Dreamwalker they would probably kill him—and they'd probably kill him slowly and painfully for pretending to be the Dreamwalker.

The only way for him to come out of this alive was for him to become this Dreamwalker. Unfortunately, the Dreamwalker was a legend he was not familiar with.

Thankfully the idea of amnesia had come to him. He did not know if this was a concept that the Comanches were familiar with, but for the moment he had convinced both Standing Stone and Tenawa, and hopefully they would be able to convince the rest of the village.

And there was another problem. He had not yet been outside

the tipi so he had no idea how large this village might be. They were far from the reservation, so they were probably stragglers who, as Tenawa had said, could not live there. If, however, the village was full strength, then he was in even more trouble, because that would mean there were that many more braves for Standing Stone to keep off him—that is, if the old man even wanted to keep them off of him. If he couldn't convince Standing Stone that he was the Dreamwalker, he wouldn't even have to worry about convincing the others.

The only Comanche Clint had ever known was Quanah Parker, and that had only been for a short while. They had come to respect each other. Clint didn't know if they had become friends, but sometimes respect was more important to an Indian than friendship. If he could not convince these Indians that he was the Dreamwalker then maybe he'd be able to convince them that he knew Quanah, and was respected by him. Clint wondered what Quanah had been doing since he had surrendered his people and brought them into the reservation. Was he even still alive? Clint had no idea.

His recovery was far from completed. He was going to have to buy himself some time until he could leave the camp feeling strong and healthy.

He would have to be completely healthy, just in case the Comanches didn't *want* him to leave the camp.

Standing Stone talked with Tenawa before she went into her tipi for the night.

"Father?"

"Yes, my daughter?"

"You believe him, don't you?"

Standing Stone's face was true to his name. It was expressionless and seemed to have been hewn from stone.

"If he is the Dreamwalker, I believe him."

"But . . . how will you know?"

"I will know."

"But how?"

"I will look at him, Daughter," Standing Stone said, "and I will know."

"Father—"

"That is enough," the shaman said. "You ask too many questions for a girl. If he is the Dreamwalker it will be made known to us."

"But if he is not—"

"Go to sleep!"

"Yes, Father."

She ducked her head and entered her tipi. Lying on her blanket she was not happy. She did not think the man she knew as Clint Adams was the Dreamwalker. A man could not be a myth. If the others found this out, she knew they would kill him. They were anxious to take their anger at the white man out on him. It was only Standing Stone, her father, who was standing between them and Clint Adams. Somehow, she had to help him convince her father that he was, indeed, the myth, the Dreamwalker.

She had to save him, for she could not bear it if he was to die.

Standing Stone remained outside, staring at the sky, long into the night. He was waiting for a sign, an answer to his questions. He knew that Bold Wolf and the others wanted to kill the white man. He knew that Tenawa did not believe that he was the Dreamwalker, but she was foolish and young. She did not believe in the old ways, the old legends, but Standing Stone did.

He would give Clint Adams every chance to convince them that he was the Dreamwalker. If he failed, Bold Wolf and the others would kill him, and Standing Stone would not be able to stop them.

So far they had left the reservation and done no harm to anyone. The old man knew that if a white man was killed, they would be hunted down and destroyed. All of Quanah's work would go for naught, but the young ones—the ones like

Bold Wolf—were so arrogant they did not even believe in the great Quanah Parker anymore.

If they did not respect Quanah, how could Standing Stone expect them to respect him?

SEVEN

Clint woke early, at first light, and sat up to test his wounds. He felt a pulling back there when he moved, but he decided to risk it. He wanted to get his first look outside before anyone realized he was awake.

He moved slowly on his hands and knees to the opening in the tipi and peered out. He looked first one way, then the other, to see if they had anyone guarding him. To his surprise, there was no one. Made bolder by this he decided to stick his head out of the flap to try to get an idea of how large the camp was.

He was very careful, looking all around as he stuck his head out, so that at the first sign of trouble he could pull his head back in again.

From his vantage point he could not see either end of the camp. It seemed, then, that he was in a fairly good-sized one. Of course, it could have been mostly women and squaws, but he wasn't willing to bet on that.

Suddenly he spotted Tenawa walking towards his tipi. He withdrew his head and carefully made his way back to his blanket. He had just settled in when the flap went up and Tenawa entered.

"You are awake."

"Yes."

"And sitting up."

He looked down at himself, smiled, and said, "So I am."

"I must look at your wounds."

"Of course. You're my nurse."

She knelt next to him and examined his wounds. When she touched him, her fingertips felt cool.

"Your touch is very pleasing," he said.

She frowned and bit her lip, settling back onto her haunches.

"You must not say such things."

"Why? Is it not fitting for the Dreamwalker to appreciate a pretty girl?"

She looked around carefully before replying.

"I know you are not the Dreamwalker," she whispered.

"You do?"

She nodded.

"How can you be so sure?" he asked, also whispering. Considering the subject, he thought whispering was a good idea.

"Because he does not exist," she said. "There is no Dreamwalker. He is a legend—no, an old wives' tale."

He digested this for a moment and then asked, "Does your father think the same thing"

"No! He believes in the old myths."

"I see. And are you going to tell him different?"

"No."

"Or the others?"

"They would kill you."

"I know," he said, with feeling.

"I do not want you to be killed."

"I feel the same way," he said. "So what do we do about it?"

"You must become the Dreamwalker."

"And how will I do that?"

"I will help you."

"How?"

"I will tell you all I know about the legend."

This was better than having to ask her to help him.

"How long do we have to make this transformation?" he asked.

"We have until you are healed."

"And when will that be?"

"When my father says it is so."

"Tenawa," he said, "why are you doing this?"

"Because I do not wish to see you killed."

"You said that before," he said. "But why?"

For her answer she reached out and touched his face, stroking his cheek. He caught her hand in his and kissed it. She was very lovely, so he drew her in and kissed her lips. Indians didn't normally kiss, so this was probably the first time for her.

"I like that," she said, with a shy smile.

"I do, too."

He kissed her again, longer, until she got the hang of it and it developed into a very good kiss.

"If your father finds out—"

"Do not worry," she said. "He believes in the Dreamwalker. He will believe in you if you remember everything that I tell you."

"Is there going to be a lot?"

"Enough," she said, "to keep you alive."

"Then I'll learn it," he said.

After Tenawa left the tipi with the promise to come back with food—and with his first lesson in becoming the Dreamwalker—Clint thought over her offer. She seemed very sincere, but he was going to have to go carefully. She was young, and could very well fall in love with him. That could end up being a big complication.

Even with her help he wondered if he'd be able to convince the old man that he was the Dreamwalker. She was young and smart, he was old and wise. She didn't believe in the legend, and Standing Stone did.

Where was the advantage? he wondered.

EIGHT

"Stealing horses is stealing power."

"I never heard that before," Clint told Tenawa. Of course he knew that stealing a man's horse in the West was a hanging offense. A horse, he knew, often meant a man's life, but he'd never heard that a horse meant power.

It did make sense, though. Any mounted army could defeat any army that was on foot. That was certainly power, wasn't it?

"Tell me more," he said.

"It is said that the shaman flies upon the back of the Horse when he dies to get to heaven."

Tenawa's English was very good, and her reference to "heaven" was further proof that she had been educated in a white man's school.

"I must tell you the story of the Dreamwalker so you will understand who you are supposed to be."

"I'm listening."

"Dreamwalker, the medicine man, was walking across the plains to the Arapaho Nation to try to heal a brother. When

31

over a rise he saw a herd of wild horses running toward him.

"Black Stallion was the first to approach him. He offered
to let Dreamwalker ride on his back to know the power of
entering darkness and finding the light. Dreamwalker promised
to return if ever his medicine was needed in the Dreamtime.

"Next a Yellow Stallion approached him."

"Yellow?" Clint asked.

She leaned forward and reminded him, "It is a legend."

"Oh, okay. Go on."

"Yellow Stallion approached and offered to take him east,
where illumination lived, so that Dreamwalker could learn the
answers and illuminate others. Dreamwalker thanked the Yellow Stallion and said that he would do so on his return journey.

"Red Stallion was next. He told Dreamwalker of the joys
of mixing work with play. He told Dreamwalker that his lessons would be better taught with humor. Dreamwalker thanked
him and promised to remember this lesson."

"Last came the White Stallion, and Dreamwalker mounted
him. The White Stallion represents wisdom. He is the message
carrier for all other horses. He said that Dreamwalker carried
the needs of his people on his back, as White Stallion carried
Dreamwalker on his. White Stallion was the symbol of a balanced medicine shield."

"What is a balanced medicine shield?"

"A shaman must have the wisdom and knowledge that has
been given by all the stallions. He must have power, wisdom,
humor. He must have all these gifts. Compassion, caring,
teaching, and loving, and he must be willing to share all of
these gifts."

"That's the shaman," Clint said. "What about the Dreamwalker?"

"Dreamwalker," Tenawa said, "is the greatest shaman of
all."

"And that's supposed to be me?"

"Yes."

"And they all think I'm Dreamwalker because of Duke?"

"Duke?"

"My horse."

"Ah, the Black Stallion."

"Well, he is black," Clint said, "but he is just a horse."

"Not to the others," Tenawa said. "They have never seen such an animal."

"Well," Clint said, "I guess I'm just lucky I didn't have a white horse."

"A White Stallion would have assured them that you were Dreamwalker," she said, "especially if you had ridden in on him."

"Next time I'll try and find one. Tell me, Tenawa, what else is there for me to learn?"

"You must learn the ways of the animals," she said. "The Bear, the Wolf, the Snake, the Horse, the Eagle, they all have powers that you must learn."

"When do those lessons start?"

"Later," she said, getting to her feet. "I have already been with you too long this time."

"When will you return?"

"I will bring you dinner," she said, "and something special."

"What?"

"You will see later," she said, and was gone.

NINE

Bold Wolf and several other young Comanche braves watched as Tenawa left the white man's tipi. Brave Wolf especially kept his eyes on her. The others were just curious about the white man, but he was in love with Tenawa. He didn't like her spending so much time with him.

"What do you say, Bold Wolf?" Running Antelope asked.

"About what?" Bold Wolf asked distractedly.

"About the white man," Little Buffalo said. "Do you think he is the Dreamwalker?"

Bold Wolf looked at them and said, "The Dreamwalker is one of the People, not a white man. No, I do not think he is the Dreamwalker."

"Then how do you explain the Black Stallion?" asked Many Horses.

It was Many Horses who had proclaimed the white man's horse to be the Black Stallion of the legends.

"I think it is a horse."

"It is a black stallion," Little Buffalo said.

"It is the Black Stallion of the legends," Many Horses said.

"It is just a horse," Bold Wolf said.

"That is not just a horse, Bold Wolf," Many Horses said. "You have seen the animal. It is not a normal horse."

"It is large," Bold Wolf said, "and it is strong, and it is probably swift, but I do not think it is the Black Stallion, just as I do not think the white man is the Dreamwalker."

"Then what would you have us do?" Running Antelope asked.

"Why would I have you do anything?"

"You led us away from the reservation," Running Antelope said, "you led us here. It is you who must tell us what to do."

"Would you listen to me or to Standing Stone about this?" Bold Wolf asked.

"Well . . . Standing Stone is the medicine man," Little Buffalo said.

"It is he who knows all about the Dreamwalker," Many Horses said.

"Then we will wait," Bold Wolf said.

"Wait for what?" Many Horses asked.

"We will wait for Standing Stone to tell us that the white man is not the Dreamwalker."

"And then what?" Many Horses asked.

"And then we will kill the white man."

"And what of his horse?"

Bold Wolf looked over to where the big black horse was standing. So far the only person who had been able to approach it was Tenawa. Others were too frightened of it.

"The horse will go to the man who kills its master," Bold Wolf said.

"I think," Running Antelope said, "you will find more men willing to try to kill the white man than you will those who would approach the Black Stallion."

"Then the animal will go to whoever can approach him safely."

"That would be Tenawa," Many Horses said, "which

means that you will get the horse when you marry her.''

"Unless one of you approaches the animal safely first,'' Bold Wolf pointed out.

He left them there to discuss it among themselves and walked to Tenawa's tipi. He intercepted her before she could enter.

"Why do you spend so much time with the white man?'' he demanded, taking her by the arm.

"He needs me.''

"Standing Stone saved his life, not you. He needs Standing Stone.''

"My father asked me to nurse him, and that is what I must do.''

"You are to marry me, Tenawa,'' Bold Wolf reminded her. "It does not look good for you to be spending so much time with the white man.''

"The white man might be the Dreamwalker.''

"Bah!'' Bold Wolf said. "That is an old wives' tale. You know it and I know it.''

"Tell that to my father, then.''

Bold Wolf released her arm and did not respond.

"Ha, you dare not.''

"I dare . . . but not yet.''

"When, then?''

"I will wait until it is obvious that the white man is not the Dreamwalker,'' Bold Wolf said. "That is when I will act.''

"That I will wait to see,'' she said, and entered her tipi.

Bold Wolf stood outside a few moments more, then looked around to see if anyone had been watching before stalking away.

Inside Tenawa hunched over, rubbing her arms. She did not want to marry Bold Wolf. It was his idea, and her father seemed to be going along with it. If, however, Bold Wolf challenged Standing Stone and was disgraced, she would not have to marry him.

She especially did not want to marry him after meeting Clint Adams. She touched her lips, where he had kissed her twice, and knew that she wanted more kisses from him . . . and more than that. . . .

TEN

"They're on the reservation," Ben Fall said.

"And I tell you I saw them," Earl Bunch said.

Bunch was riding point for the three men so they wouldn't run headlong into a posse, or an army patrol, just so they'd be ready for anything.

Now he claimed he saw Indians.

"What kind of Indians were they?" Fall asked.

"How the hell do I know what kind they were?" Bunch asked. "What do I look like, an Indian agent? I don't know one Indian from the next."

"I think you're crazy—"

"I know Indians when I see them—"

"You just said you didn't know an Indian from a hole in the ground—"

"I said I didn't know one Indian from another."

Their arguments were overlapping, but Tucker Spring was ignoring them. He was looking off at the horizon.

"Whataya think, Tuck?" Fall asked. "Is he crazy or what?"

"I saw—"

"Could be Comanches."

"What?" Fall asked.

"I said he could be right," Spring said, "and they could be Comanches from the reservation in Oklahoma."

"Well, if they belong on the reservation," Fall asked, "what the hell are they doin' here?"

Spring looked at Fall and said, "Maybe they didn't like it on the reservation."

"Well, ain't it against the law or somethin' for them to leave?"

"That's right," Spring said, "if they left they broke the law. I guess we should find some law and turn them in, huh, Ben?"

Fall looked away, disgusted that Spring had made a fool of him, and he saw Bunch grinning.

"What are you smilin' at?"

"Nothin'," Bunch said, trying to hide the smile but only succeeding in turning it into a smirk.

"How many did you see?" Spring asked.

"About five."

"Five," Fall said, with a derisive snort. "We can take care of five."

"Where there's five," Spring said, "there's bound to be more."

"What do you suggest, then?" Fall asked.

"We'd better change our direction," Spring said.

"On his say-so?" Fall demanded, pointing at Bunch.

"He says he saw Indians, Ben," Spring said. "If you don't believe him, then you keep heading west."

"What are you gonna do?"

"Head north."

"North! Why don't we head south? We're only two days ride from New Mexico."

"You're wanted in New Mexico, Ben," Spring said, "or did you forget about a certain saloon girl and her boyfriend, who you killed?"

"I didn't kill the girl," Fall said, "I only killed the boyfriend. How many times I gotta tell people? He killed the girl."

"Oh, that's right," Spring said, "you killed him because he killed her."

"No, no," Bunch said, "he killed him because he called him short, Tuck, remember?"

"Oh, yeah, now I remember," Spring said.

"Shut up, Bunch!"

"Come on, Earl," Spring said, "we'll head north while Ben, here, heads south."

"Okay, okay," Fall said, "I'm headin' north with you. It's just that it's a long ways to either Nebraska or Wyoming, and we got to go back the way we came."

"We'll have to take the chance," Spring said.

ELEVEN

Over the course of the next few days Clint worked closely with Tenawa on his Dreamwalker lessons. He learned many things that the Indians believed about animals that he had not known before, and he found it fascinating.

He had already learned about the horse and how the animal was the symbol of power—physical power and unearthly power.

She told him that the Indians honored each living thing as a teacher.

"Each animal teaches a lesson," Tenawa told him. "The Wolf, especially, is a teacher. He is also a pathfinder. He teaches us to share medicine. The Wolf mates for life, and so he teaches us about love, trust, and generosity."

"All that in a wolf?" Clint said, shaking his head. "What about the Eagle?" He was getting into the spirit of the lessons.

"The Eagle is the power of the Great Spirit. His feathers are a tool of healing."

Clint vaguely remembered something touching his back which, at the time, he had thought of as a ''featherlike'' touch.

"He is the symbol of initiation."

"Initiation into what?"

"The ways of life. The Eagle tells us that we must experience great sorrow as well as great joy in our life. Only then can we be complete. He also teaches us to look higher until we can touch Grandfather Sun with our hearts. He is sacred because only he can fly high enough to take messages to our Creator."

He knew she didn't mean God when she said Creator, not the white man's God, anyway.

"Tell me about the Bear," he said, and for a moment a picture of the bear that had attacked him flashed into his mind.

"The Bear teaches us to look inside ourselves for answers. He hibernates, and while sleeping he seeks answers in his dreams. When he wakes in the spring it is as if he is reborn."

"Well, then, that must have been a reborn bear that attacked me."

"Either it was not a sacred bear," she said, "or it was, and the attack is something that you are supposed to learn from."

"Yeah, I learned that bears can be pretty quiet when they want to."

"Then there is the Snake."

"You can learn something from a snake?" he asked, surprised again. He thought snakes were just something you learned to avoid.

"The shedding of the Snake's skin is a lesson in life, death, and being reborn," she explained. "Some tribes, like the Hopi, believe that the Snake brings messages from beyond, and brings life-giving rains. The Ojibwa have a Snake Clan which is a medicine clan. They believe the Snake represents patience."

Clint could believe that. He had seen for himself how a snake could sit on a rock, coiled and ready to strike and wait that way for hours. That had been once when he was in a ravine, himself waiting patiently for hours.

"He is patient because he is slow to anger," Tenawa went on. "He is also a symbol of female powers, and of healing."

She told him about the Dog, who would often give warnings of impending danger. Dogs helped hunt, and were a source of warmth on cold nights. The Dog represented great loyalty.

She told him of the Mountain Lion, which taught great lessons of leadership. By watching this animal you learned how to balance power, physical strength, and grace.

"The Elk is stamina. He cannot defeat the Mountain Lion who seeks to kill and devour him, so he outruns it.

"The Deer is gentleness.

"The Moose is self-esteem.

"The Coyote is the trickster.

"For years the great Buffalo gave my people sustenance," she said, "so the Buffalo is the symbol of prayer and gratitude."

She talked to him of many more animals after that but the ones he retained more knowledge of were these five: the Horse, the Snake, the Wolf, the Bear, and the Eagle. They were certainly the ones he had come in contact with more than any other, and they were not victims, like the Deer and the Rabbit and the Turkey.

"Tomorrow," she said, standing up as it got late, "we will talk about the Medicine Wheel. There is still much you must know if you are to become the Dreamwalker."

"Wait, Tenawa," Clint said, grabbing her wrist but holding it gently, "stay and talk with me a few minutes more."

"About what?"

"About your father, about the others," he said. "Are they growing impatient with me?"

"With you," she said, "and with Standing Stone."

"I truly do not want to bring trouble to your father, Tenawa."

"I know you do not."

"Who must I impress, besides him?"

"If you impressed Bold Wolf you would win over everyone," she said.

"Is he the leader?"

"He would like to be a leader. He is young. He took us

from the reservation and brought us this far, but he is not yet a great leader."

"But the others look to him?"

"Yes."

"So if I can persuade him that I am the Dreamwalker I'll be okay?"

"It will not be easy."

"Why?"

"He does not like you. He wants to kill you."

"Because I'm white."

"And because he wants to marry me." She slid her hand from his loose grip and said, "I will see you in the morning."

Clint stared after her and then shook his head. The way his luck was going this figured. First he gets attacked by a bear, then he gets robbed—he hadn't forgotten about *that*—and then some young brave wants to kill him because he wants to marry the medicine man's daughter, who is nursing him back to health.

What else could go wrong?

TWELVE

Standing Stone came out of his tipi and found Bold Wolf there.

"I want to talk," the younger man said.

"About what?" the medicine man asked.

"About Tenawa," Bold Wolf said, "and the white man."

"What about them?"

"She is spending too much time with him."

"So?"

"She is supposed to marry me," Bold Wolf complained. "It does not look right."

"My daughter has a mind of her own, Bold Wolf," Standing Stone said. "Why come to me with your problem? You must speak with her."

"I have spoken with her."

"And you have not gotten anywhere, eh?"

"She does not respect me."

"Perhaps not."

"You did not raise her right, Standing Stone. She is supposed to be respectful."

47

"She is respectful to me," the older man said. "Perhaps you have not yet earned her respect."

"Old man—"

Standing Stone held his hand up and Bold Wolf stopped. As badly as Bold Wolf wanted to be a leader, and to be respected, he knew that Standing Stone *was* respected by everyone in camp and, grudgingly, he respected the older man, himself.

"I will speak no more of Tenawa."

"All right," Bold Wolf said, "then we will speak of the white man."

"What about him?"

"Has he yet proven himself to be the Dreamwalker?"

"I have not yet asked for proof."

"Why not?"

"He has not yet recovered from his wounds."

"Would not the Dreamwalker have already recovered?"

"Have you ever met the Dreamwalker?" Standing Stone asked.

"Of course I have not."

"Neither have I," the older man said. "So I do not know if he would have already recovered or not."

"Yes, but if—"

"And if the Dreamwalker is residing inside the body of a normal man then he would recover as a normal man would . . . slowly."

"If the Dreamwalker would inhabit the body of a normal man," Bold Wolf said, "would it not be the body of one of the People?"

"I do not know," Standing Stone said. "If this is indeed the Dreamwalker, then I will ask him why he chose a white man."

"This man is *not* the Dreamwalker," Bold Wolf insisted. "The sooner you realize that, the sooner we can deal with him."

"The identity of this man will be made known to me in

time," Standing Stone said. "Until that happens he will not be harmed. Is that clear?"

"You are not the leader here," Bold Wolf said.   -

"I am the oldest," Standing Stone said. "Sometimes that is where the leadership lies."

"Not this time," Bold Wolf said. "I lead here."

"Then do what you will," Standing Stone said, waving at the tipi Clint Adams was in, "and let the consequences of the Dreamwalker be on your head."

With that Standing Stone walked away from the younger man, leaving Bold Wolf speechless.

Standing Stone knew that the young Comanche did not have the courage yet to challenge the old legends. It might only be a matter of days, though, before he could muster the courage. By that time the shaman wanted to know who the white man really was so he would know what to do when Bold Wolf came for him.

THIRTEEN

Lt. Kenneth McLain of the Fourth Cavalry watched as his point man, Winston Guest, came riding back to him and his company.

It was McLain's job to track down the Comanches who had left the reservation and bring them back. To do this he had been given a company of twenty men, because of the forty Comanches who had fled, twenty-five of them were women, children, and old men. Only about a dozen of them were young braves, but braves who were not experienced in battle. It was thought that a company this size would be plenty to bring them back.

Guest was not in the Army, but he was paid by the Army as a civilian scout.

"He doesn't look happy," Sergeant Rick Henderson said to his commanding officer.

"No, Sergeant, he doesn't."

As it turned out, Winston Guest was not a happy man. He had not been able to pick up the trail of the Comanches since he'd lost it two days earlier, and he was feeling more and more embarrassed by this fact.

"Well, Mr. Guest?" McLain asked.

"I'm sorry, sir," McLain said, "there is still no sign of them."

"How could this be?" McLain asked. "Forty Comanches, most of them women and children? How could they move without leaving a trail?"

"They do have Standing Stone with them, sir."

McLain snorted and said, "A washed-out old man."

"Not so, sir," Guest said. "Standing Stone is a respected elder, and he has the experience—"

"An old man has the experience to go undetected by you, Mr. Guest? I understood that you, yourself, were supposed to be a man of some experience, sir."

Guest was forty-five years old and had been a mountain man, an Indian fighter, and a scout for the Army. He was, indeed, an experienced man, which was why he was so puzzled by the ability of these Comanches to avoid him.

"I am, sir."

"Then, Mr. Guest, I suggest you find me those Comanches before I decide to have you replaced."

Speaking of experience, Guest knew that the thirty-year-old lieutenant had little of his own when dealing with Comanches, but at the moment he didn't think it prudent to point that out.

"Yes, sir," he said. "I'll do my best."

"I had thought you were already, Mr. Guest."

Guest bit his lip, turned his horse, and rode off.

"You're pushin' him, sir," Sergeant Henderson said. He was in his forties and had more experience than his commander in almost every aspect of the military.

"Am I, Sergeant?"

"Yes, sir," Henderson said. "Guest is as good as they come. If the Comanches are eluding him, it's because somebody with them is good, too."

McLain turned his head and gave the sergeant a lazy look.

"Sergeant, when I want your opinion on something I will ask for it. Is that clear?"

Henderson stared at McLain for just a split second, then

jerked his eyes front and said, "Yes, sir!" very loudly.

McLain then raised his gloved hand, shouted, "Forward!" and led the way.

Henderson hesitated just a moment while Private Alan Russell rode up next to him.

"What do you think?" Russell asked.

"I think our young lieutenant's got more sand than brains, that's what I think," Henderson said.

"He keeps pushing Guest and he's gonna run out of sand," Russell said.

In spite of himself Henderson let a small smile creep in and said, "That might be worth the price of admission, don't you think?"

FOURTEEN

The next day when Tenawa came to his tipi with his breakfast Clint said, "I would like to go for a walk."

She looked dubious.

"I do not think that is wise."

"Why not? You said yourself that my wounds are healing well. I'll walk slowly."

"It is not just your wounds I am worried about."

"Then what is it? Bold Wolf?"

She hesitated, then said, "Yes . . . and the others."

"Tenawa, I'll bet that everyone in your camp is curious about me."

"Yes, they are."

"Well, why not give them a look at me?" he suggested. "And at the same time I can take a look at my horse."

She frowned.

"I do not think—"

"I'm determined."

She stared at him and then said, "All right—but only after you eat."

"Agreed."

• • •

When the fresh air hit his face Clint stopped short and took
a deep breath.

"Are you all right?" she asked.

"I'm fine," he said, "it's just been a long time since I was
outside."

He knew it had been a matter of days but it felt like he'd
been cooped up inside for months.

"Show me the camp," he said.

"All right."

As they walked she stayed right next to him, supporting
him. His back felt tight and there was some pain, but he was
determined to walk awhile and get his legs back under him.
If he moved slowly enough there'd be no danger of the
wounds opening up again.

He saw women cooking and doing laundry and making
clothes and moccasins. He saw children at play and old men
sitting around smoking. He did not see any young men.

"Where are Bold Wolf and the others?"

"They are hunting," she said. "They will be back later."

Clint wondered what they were hunting for. Since they had
left the reservation there would probably be a company of
soldiers out looking for them. Were the young men trying to
find themselves a battle to fight?

"Where is your father?"

"He is in his tipi," she said, "trying to communicate with
the great spirits."

"Trying to communicate with the Dreamwalker?"

"He believes that the Dreamwalker is inside you."

"Does he really?"

"Yes, he does."

They came to a water hole where about a dozen children
were either bathing or just splashing around. They watched
them for a while until the children noticed them. At that point
they stopped splashing and stared at Clint with wide eyes. He
knew it wasn't that he was white, because on the reservation
they had probably seen a lot of white men. They were staring

at him in awe and wonder because they had heard that he was
the Dreamwalker.

"Do they know the legend?"

"Yes," Tenawa said. "They have been told the stories by
the elders."

Clint wondered if he should smile and wave at them, then
went ahead and did it. To his surprise most of them responded
by smiling and waving back. Tenawa also laughed and waved.

"They were suffocating on the reservation," she said, as
they continued walking. "This is where they should grow up,
out in the open."

"You grew up on the reservation, didn't you?"

"Yes."

"And you feel you missed something?"

"I feel as if I grew up in prison, and now I am free," she
said.

"Whose idea was it to leave?"

"The young ones," she said. "Bold Wolf, Many Horses,
and the others. Anyone who wanted to follow them was wel-
come."

"And many did?"

"There are forty-three of us," she said.

"How many young braves like Bold Wolf?"

"Maybe twelve."

"That's not many," Clint said. "What will happen when
the Army catches up with you?"

"Maybe they will not come after us." Her tone was hope-
ful.

"You don't believe that."

She hesitated, then said, "No."

"These braves are inexperienced," he said. "If they fight
they'll be killed."

"Yes."

"And the rest of you will be taken back."

"Yes."

"If Bold Wolf wants to marry you, maybe you can talk to
him."

"About what?"

"About going back before the Army catches you."

She shook her head.

"Bold Wolf and the others would rather die out here than go back to the reservation."

"And what about the children? And the old ones? They might die, too."

"The Army would not kill them. Or the women."

"Tenawa, I'm sure you've heard stories about entire villages being burned, the people killed."

"Yes, but those things happened many years ago, during a war."

"For some white men the war with the Indians never ends."

She looked down at the ground and said, "For some Indians it is the same."

Clint turned slowly then to look behind them and saw that some of the children from the water hole were following them.

"We have company."

She turned and looked, then smiled.

"They are fascinated by you," she said. "They look at you the way they look at your horse."

"Where is Duke, by the way?"

"Just up ahead."

They walked a few yards more and then the horses came into view. There were only a few of them, since the younger braves were out on their hunting party. Duke was standing off by himself, not tethered as the others were. As Clint approached, the gelding's huge head came up. Tenawa stayed back, and the children stayed back even further.

Duke's nostrils flared as Clint reached him, which was a great display of emotion for the big horse.

"Hiya, big fella," Clint said, patting his massive neck. He examined Duke critically and saw that he was in excellent condition. Tenawa had been feeding him. All he needed was to be brushed and rubbed down and he'd look as good as new.

"These people all think that you and I are something special," he said, rubbing the gelding's nose. "Well, they're right about you, but I don't know about me. Actually, they think you're pretty magic.''

Clint looked over at Tenawa and saw that the children had moved closer and were now gathered around her.

''Look at them,'' Clint said to Duke. ''They're expecting me to jump on your back and both of us to fly away. Too bad we can't, huh, big boy?''

Clint stood there a moment, studying Tenawa and the children, their faces even more awestruck than before.

''Whataya say, big fella?'' he asked Duke. ''Should we give them a thrill?''

Clint leaned into Duke's mouth so the children would think the big, black gelding was talking to him.

''Come on,'' Clint said, ''let's give them a closer look.''

FIFTEEN

As Clint walked toward Tenawa and the children, Duke followed behind him. Seeing this the children started to back up, and even the girl seemed unsure about what to do, although she'd been the closest to the horse all this time.

"Wait," Clint called, and the kids all stopped. "Stay there."

They listened to him, because he was Dreamwalker, the legend.

Clint continued toward them with Duke trailing behind. When he reached them he stopped, and the horse stopped and stood patiently.

"Would you like to take a closer look at the Black Stallion?" Clint asked the children.

They all stared.

Tenawa turned and said something to them in their own language. Several of them continued to stare, but for the most part they all nodded with wide eyes.

"Tell them to come closer," Clint said to Tenawa.

She relayed the message and the children began to shuffle

forward slowly. Most of them were looking at Duke but some of them were staring at Clint, too. What were they looking for? he wondered. Wings? On either of them? Or both?

Clint instructed the children, through Tenawa, to walk around Duke but not to touch him. The big gelding had never really been around a lot of children before. He knew that Duke would stand fast and not move, but he didn't know how the big gelding would react to having a dozen pair of little hands all over him.

The children were overcome by the sheer size of the horse, something Clint sometimes took for granted. He was struck by it now, seeing the children surrounding the horse, how he dwarfed them.

"Stop!"

The single word, spoken loudly but not shouted, did just that. It stopped everyone right in their tracks.

Clint turned his head and saw Standing Stone. The children saw him, too, and they didn't move. Tenawa turned, saw him, and walked over to him. They had a conversation where the medicine man did most of the talking. Finally, Tenawa hung her head for a moment, then turned and walked back to where Clint and the children were. She spoke briefly to the children, who all looked crestfallen and started walking away slowly.

"What's going on?" Clint asked.

"My father says that the Black Stallion should not be put on display. He is to be respected."

"They weren't being disrespectful."

"It does not matter," she said. "He wants them to go back to what they were doing."

Clint looked over at Standing Stone, who was staring at him.

"Does he want to talk to me?"

"No," she said, "not yet."

"Then when?"

"Tonight."

"Why tonight?"

"He says that since you are walking around you must be

well enough to remember who you are.''

Uh-oh, Clint thought.

''I tried to tell him that you are not, but he does not think that I am a proper judge.''

''Am I ready?''

''No,'' she said, ''there is still much to learn.''

''Well,'' he said, ''I'd better take Duke back to where he was and we can get busy teaching me the rest of it.''

''By tonight?''

He nodded and said, ''By tonight. I don't see that I have that much of a choice, do you?''

SIXTEEN

When they went back to the tipi, Tenawa told Clint about the Medicine Wheel. It was used to set up a sacred ceremonial place. It was constructed by placing twelve stones in a circle, with the four largest stones north, south, east, and west.

"Like a clock," Clint said.

She looked at him blankly.

"A clock," he said. "What white men use to tell time? Like a watch?"

"Oh, yes." She had seen watches on some of the white men around the reservation.

"With the largest stones at twelve, three, six, and nine," Clint said, for his own benefit.

"All right," she said. If that was the way he could remember it, that was fine with her.

"You must place the stones beginning with the south, which is the place of the child. This is where life begins. Then you move to the west, the north, and finally, the east. The spirit enters the circle through the eastern door."

She explained that the Medicine Wheel was used to gather

the energies of all the animals they had talked about. The ceremony was a way of honoring and recognizing the connections to all life, and of showing gratitude through dances and chants and rituals, all of which were performed with the guidance of the Great Spirit.

She taught him about the Stone People, Mother Earth, Father Sky, Grandfather Sun, Grandmother Moon, the Sky World, the Standing People—also known as the trees—the Two Leggeds—people—the Sky Brothers and Sisters, and the Thunder People. These, she said, were all relatives.

She explained how the Medicine Wheel was the wheel of life, constantly revolving and bringing new truths and new lessons to the walking of the path.

In the end she said that the Medicine Wheel was life, afterlife, rebirth, and the honoring of each step taken along the way.

It all made sense to him, which was going to make it easier to remember.

"This is all very beautiful, Tenawa."

"You must remember all of it."

"Actually, I've thought about that."

"About what?"

"About whether or not I need to remember it all," he said. "I've already explained to Standing Stone that my memory was affected by my injury. What if my memory came back slowly, little by little? What if I remembered about the animals, but not about the wheel yet? Or the other way around? Do you think he'd accept that?"

"Possibly," she said, "but what about later?"

"Well, I'll give him what you've taught me little by little," he explained, "and let him think that my memory is coming back that way."

She thought it over and then said, "My father is not easy to fool."

"But we're trying, aren't we?"

"We must," she said, "or you will be killed."

"Well, that's a good enough reason to try."

"Clint, after today it would not be easy for you to try and leave."

"Why not? They haven't been watching me that closely."

"You were seen walking around today," she said. "I am sure Bold Wolf will have someone watching you—guarding you—from now on."

"That's great."

"It is?"

"I was being sarcastic."

"I learned about sar-casm," she said, remembering. "White men use it all the time."

"Yes, they do. It means I was foolish not to have tried to leave earlier."

"You could not, because of your injury."

"Then I was foolish not to listen to you earlier today, when you told me not to go for a walk."

"Men do not usually listen to women when they talk."

"Did you learn that in a white man's school?"

"It is the same everywhere," she said, with a shrug.

She walked to the entrance of the tipi.

SEVENTEEN

After Tenawa left, Clint didn't know how much time he'd have before Standing Stone appeared. He started going over his "lessons" in his mind, but he kept wandering off the subject.

For one thing he was thinking about the three men who had robbed him. He wasn't about to forget how they'd treated him when he was helpless, and then left him to die. He was going to have to get on their trail pretty quickly, though, before it dried up. That meant getting away from these Comanches, and that meant convincing the shaman that he was the Dreamwalker, and that took him right back to his lessons.

He was going to have to go ahead with his plan to convince Standing Stone that he was slowly regaining his memory. Maybe he could stretch what Tenawa had taught him to a few days, so he'd only have to remember pieces of it at a time. Once he convinced Standing Stone, and the shaman convinced the rest of the camp, then maybe he'd be able to leave.

Once he was gone he didn't know what he'd do about the Comanches. True, they had left the reservation and were probably being hunted even now, but they had saved his life. He wouldn't feel comfortable giving their location away, to the Army or anyone.

It occurred to him then that he didn't really know what the three men had stolen from him, because he didn't know where anything was. Surely they must have taken his money, but what of his saddle, saddlebags, rifle, and pistol? Were they being kept somewhere by the Comanches, or had the three white men made off with them as well? He'd have to remember to ask Tenawa the next time she came to him.

He found himself wishing that he had met the Indian girl under other circumstances. She was lovely, and smart, and compassionate. He was sorry that she'd had to grow up on a reservation, and even more sorry that she was now on the run. He wished there was some way he could help her.

She had told him that Bold Wolf wanted to marry her, but she didn't say anything about wanting to marry him. He knew that Indian women rarely had any say regarding who they married. Love often had little to do with it. A young brave wanted a strong young wife to bear his children and keep him happy. The girl's father wanted the horses or blankets or whatever was being traded for the girl. He wondered if this was the case with Standing Stone. How did he feel about Bold Wolf as a prospective son-in-law?

Clint was surprised when the tipi flap opened and Standing Stone entered. He had thought the man would come much later.

It was time for him to perform.

The old man sat opposite Clint and stared at him for a long time. Clint was amazed that nothing on the man's face moved. He did not even seem to blink his eyes.

Finally, unable to stand the silence anymore, Clint said, "What is it?"

"Begin."

"Begin what?"

"Talk," Standing Stone said.

"About what?"

"Convince me that you are the Dreamwalker."

"What do you want me to tell you?"

Standing Stone looked away, as if Clint was not even worth a glance.

"The Dreamwalker would know what to tell me."

What should he do? Clint wondered. Start spouting the stuff Tenawa had taught him? Or play it a different way?

He decided to play it the way he would if he was knee-deep in a poker hand and didn't have any good cards to play with.

He was going to bluff.

EIGHTEEN

"Would the Dreamwalker perform for you?" he asked.
"Like some trained animal?"

Slowly, Standing Stone's eyes moved until he and Clint were looking at each other.

"I think you should look at the wounds on my back, shaman," Clint said, as coldly as he could.

Standing Stone stared at him for a long time and for a moment Clint thought he had overplayed his hand. Finally, the old man moved, getting to his feet, walking over to Clint, kneeling by him and examining the wounds on his back.

"You heal very well," he said.

"You did your job well, shaman."

Standing Stone finished his examination and returned to his seated position across from Clint.

"Tomorrow I would like something to wear," Clint said. "A shirt."

"I will see to it."

"How long have you been camped here?"

Standing Stone thought a moment then held up three fingers and said, "Three weeks."

"If you stay in one place any longer the Army will catch up to you."

"We stayed," Standing Stone said, "to see to your wounds."

Clint didn't know if that was true. Did they think, from the first moment they brought him in, that he might be the Dreamwalker? Thanks to Duke, they finally did. If these people were caught and returned to the reservation, or worse, it would be his fault.

"I think you should move tomorrow," Clint said.

Standing Stone thought this over, then nodded slowly.

"You will travel with us?"

"Of course," Clint said. If he had suggested leaving him behind, then that *would* have been overplaying his hand. At the very least the younger braves probably wouldn't have gone for that idea.

"You are not ready to ride."

"I will walk then," Clint said. "Walking is not unusual for the Dreamwalker, is it?"

"No," Standing Stone said, "it is not."

"I am growing tired now," Clint said. "If you want to talk to me more it will have to wait until tomorrow, after we have relocated and I have rested from the journey."

Standing Stone stared at Clint for a long time, and he couldn't tell what the old shaman was thinking. Eventually, the man stood up and left without another word.

How arrogant would the Dreamwalker be? Clint wondered. He wished he knew.

NINETEEN

After Standing Stone left, Clint heaved a sigh of relief. By going on the offensive he had bought himself a little time. Indians respected strength, and he had shown strength not only by standing up to the shaman, but by suggesting that they all move the camp tomorrow. He knew he wasn't ready for a long trek, but by suggesting it he had impressed Standing Stone. Also, by not performing as the shaman had wanted him to— by trying to "convince" him that he was the Dreamwalker— he had gained even more respect.

But the respect had been gained from Standing Stone. What would happen when the shaman told the others that they were going to break camp and move?

"Who says we must move?" Bold Wolf demanded.

Standing Stone had sent for Bold Wolf, Many Horses, and the other young braves.

"We have been here too long already," Standing Stone said.

"Who says this?" Bold Wolf demanded again.

Standing Stone inclined his head toward Clint's tipi and said, "He says it."

Bold Wolf pointed at the tipi and demanded, "When did he become the leader?"

"He is not the leader," Standing Stone said, "but he is right. If we stay here any longer, the white soldiers will find us and take us back to the reservation."

"They will not take me back," Many Horses said. "I will fight them to the death."

"To the death of our squaws and our children?" Standing Stone asked. "It is better that we keep moving."

"So says he?" Bold Wolf demanded.

"I think Standing Stone is right," Little Buffalo said. "It is better if we break camp and continue on."

"Continue to where?" Bold Wolf asked. "Where is there to go?"

"You should have thought of that before you convinced us to go," Standing Stone said.

Bold Wolf glared at the old man.

"What do you think, Running Antelope?" Many Horses asked.

"I think we should go."

"Little Buffalo?"

"We go."

They asked some of the other young braves and they all agreed.

Lastly, they looked at Bold Wolf.

"Why ask me?" he demanded in disgust. "You have all made up your minds."

He dismissed them all with a contemptuous wave of his hand and stormed off.

"He will go with us," Many Horses said.

"Then in the morning we break camp," Standing Stone said.

"Is the Dream—is the white man able to ride?" Many Horses asked.

"Not yet."

"Then how will he travel?"

"He says he will walk."

"If he walks," Running Antelope said, "I will walk, too."

"And I," Little Buffalo said.

"And I, as well," Many Horses said.

"Very well," Standing Stone said. "Tell the others that they must be ready to move by the time of the first sunlight."

The young men dispersed to do that. Standing Stone walked to Tenawa's tipi and called her out.

"What is it, Father?"

"Tomorrow we break camp."

"To go where?"

"To go," he said, with a shrug. "If we stay here the soldiers will catch us."

"But he is not ready to travel," she said, looking over at Clint's tent.

"Moving was his idea, Daughter," Standing Stone said.

"You have talked to him tonight?"

"I have."

"And did he convince you that he was the Dreamwalker?" she asked excitedly.

Standing Stone hesitated and then said, "Let us say he made a convincing start."

He turned, started to walk away, then turned back.

"He will need something to wear," Standing Stone said. "A shirt."

"I have made him one," she said.

"Then take it to him."

Tenawa intended to take it to him, and tonight. She wanted to hear what went on between her father and Clint Adams that had resulted in the entire camp moving in the morning.

Clint looked up when Tenawa entered the tipi.

"I have brought you a shirt," she said. "I made it myself."

She handed it to him and he saw that it was made of buckskin. It was very soft to the touch, and he knew that she had worked very hard to get it that way.

"What happened with you and my father?"

"Why?"

"He has told everyone that we are moving tomorrow," she said.

"That's good."

"Is it true? It was your idea?"

"Yes."

"Why?"

"If we stay here and all of you are caught and sent back it would be my fault."

"Why would you not want us to be caught? You would be safe then."

He touched her face and said, "I don't want you to have to go back to the reservation if you don't want to, Tenawa."

She leaned into the touch of his hand and, in a daring move, touched his face with her hand.

"When you leave," she said, "I would like to go with you."

"And I would like to take you," he found himself saying—and meaning it. He wanted to take her someplace where she could live in peace. "But for now, I must stay with your people."

"What did you tell my father?"

He told her that he had acted arrogantly when he was instructed to perform. She laughed as he described the look on her father's face.

"You were wonderful," she said, and leaned into him, putting her head against his chest.

He put his hand behind her head, beneath her hair, and touched the back of her neck. She sighed and he found that his hand easily fit inside her dress. He ran his hand down over the smooth skin of her back. She shifted so that she could pull her dress up so that she wasn't sitting on it. He took the opportunity to slide his other hand beneath the dress. He touched her belly and she flinched. He moved his hand higher and cupped one breast with his hand. Her breast was round and firm, and her nipple hardened against his palm. He then rubbed his hand over both breasts as she moaned and leaned against him.

He slid one hand beneath her then, cupping one naked cheek, sliding his finger along the cleft between her buttocks.

She moaned and then said, "Please." The single word needed no explanation.

Knowing he might be wrong, and that he definitely was taking a chance, he eased her away from him so he could undo his pants. She helped him slide them down and discard them, then pulled her dress up over her head. Naked, she sat in his lap.

She slid her arms around his neck and was very careful to keep her hands away from his wounds. He kissed her, forcing her mouth open, and then slid his mouth down over her throat until he was kissing her breasts, rolling her nipples between his lips.

He slid his hands beneath her, cupped both cheeks of her buttocks, lifted her and then lowered her onto him. She was wet, and he slid into her easily. She groaned as she took him fully.

"You must sit still," she said in his ear. "Let me . . ."

He knew she was right. If he tried to move too much he was going to open his wounds. He sat still then as she rode up and down on him, biting her lip to keep from crying out. As still as he was, though, his hands moved over her, touching her, caressing her, pinching her, sliding over and, at times, in and out of her as she continued to ride him. Perspiration started to slide down her body in droplets. Soon he, too, was sweating, even though she was doing all of the work.

She braced her hands first against his chest and then his belly as she moved over him, and then suddenly she came down on him and stayed that way. Her eyes closed tightly, she bit her lip even harder, and then she was shuddering. He held her tightly and then she started to move again, up and down on him slowly, and then faster and faster until he could hold back no longer and he exploded inside of her. . . .

• • •

"Tenawa," he whispered, "you must go."

She lifted her head, which had been resting on his chest, so that she spoke into his neck.

"I do not want to go." She put her arms around his neck. "I want to stay with you." She was still very breathless from the encounter.

He kissed the top of her head and reached for her dress.

"You know you can't," he said. "Not tonight."

"No," she said, moving away, "not tonight. It would be dangerous for you."

"And you."

It had already been dangerous for both of them. Someone could have walked in on them at any time, and if it had been Standing Stone or Bold Wolf they would have been in trouble—him more than her.

"Another time," she said sadly.

He lifted her chin with his hand and kissed her mouth. She stood up and slipped her dress back on, then helped him back into his pants.

"Definitely another time," he said.

She smiled, then rose and left quickly, before she could change her mind.

TWENTY

Clint was glad Tenawa had left. Another moment of her silky skin beneath his hands and he wouldn't have let her. He could still feel her hard nipples against his palms.

He was looking down at the shirt she had made for him when he heard someone enter. He thought it was her, returning, but when he looked up it was someone he had never seen before.

"You are not the Dreamwalker," the young brave said, pointing a finger at him.

"I'm not?"

"No. The Dreamwalker would not appear to us in the body of a white man."

"Have you seen the Dreamwalker before?"

"I—no, I have not."

"Then how would you know?"

The brave just glared at him.

"You must be Bold Wolf."

"You know me?"

"I know of you."

Bold Wolf stood up straight and puffed out his chest.

"What have you heard?"

"That soon you will be a great leader."

"When?"

"When you are older."

"Bah," Bold Wolf said, "leadership is for the young, not the old."

"Not when you are old," Clint said, "Just when you are older. You must wait. You still have much to learn."

For a moment Clint thought he was going to get away with it, but then the confused look left Bold Wolf's face and was replaced by something else.

"You cannot fool me, white man," he said. "You are not the Dreamwalker. I will never believe that."

"You can believe what you wish."

"And I want you to stay away from Tenawa. She is mine." He pounded his chest to make his point clear.

"Is that what she says?"

"It is what I say."

"And what does Standing Stone say?"

"Standing Stone is an old man. I have warned you, white man."

With that he left, leaving behind his threats and his distrust and his contempt, all of which hung thick in the air.

Clint was glad the young man had only come to talk. He doubted that in his weakened state he would have been able to defend himself if the brave had wanted to do more.

TWENTY-ONE

When Bunch came riding back to Spring and Fall he did not look happy.

"What is it now?" Spring asked.

"Soldiers."

"How many?"

"Twenty, maybe more."

"Lookin' for us?" Fall asked, looking at Bunch.

"I doubt it. We ain't wanted hereabouts."

"Then what?"

Spring thought a moment.

"They're lookin' for those Indians Bunch saw."

"That must be it," Bunch agreed.

"Did they see you?" Spring asked.

"No . . . I don't think so."

Spring looked at the sky.

"It'll be dark soon. Let's find a place to camp for the night."

"Shouldn't we keep movin', stay ahead of them?"

"They comin' this way, Bunch?"

"I think so."

"You *think* so?" Fall repeated. "You *think* they didn't see you. Don't you *know* nothin'?"

"I know more than you do—"

"Shut up, the both of you," Spring said. He didn't shout, or even snap, he just said it conversationally, and they both fell silent. "We'll camp. If they catch up with us we'll just tell them what they want to know."

"What's that?" Bunch asked.

"Where you saw those Indians, stupid," Fall said.

"Don't call me that . . ."

Spring turned his horse and rode off, ignoring both of them. He knew they'd eventually realize he'd gone and hurry to catch up to him.

And if they didn't, would that be so bad?

Lt. Kenneth McLain sat in his saddle and surveyed the surrounding area.

"They're out there."

"How can you tell, sir?" Sergeant Rick Henderson asked.

McLain answered without looking at his sergeant. It was just as well. He wouldn't have liked the look on the man's face when he said, "I can smell 'em."

The only place Lt. McLain had ever seen an Indian was on the reservation, and he'd never said anything then about being able to smell them. Henderson doubted the man would be able to smell an Indian who was standing right next to him.

"Rider comin'," a trooper called out.

McLain jerked his head about, looking for the rider, which Henderson found even funnier. The lieutenant claimed he could smell an Indian, but he couldn't see an approaching rider.

"He's right there, sir—" Henderson started, but the lieutenant cut him off.

"I see him, Sergeant," he said testily.

"Yes, sir."

It was the scout, Winston Guest, coming back.

"Well?" McLain said as Guest reined his horse in.

"I think they're camped someplace, sir."

"Why do you say that?"

"There are no fresh tracks anywhere. If they're hunting, they're doing it north of here and we haven't crossed those tracks yet."

"You didn't see anything?"

"I didn't say that, sir. I did see some tracks, but they're made by shod horses."

"White men?"

"Yes, sir."

"How many?"

"Three."

"Traveling in what direction?"

"Well, north now."

"What do you mean?"

"Well, judging by their tracks they were goin' south, but then they reversed their direction."

"Why?"

Guest gave Henderson a fleeting look, then said to McLain, "I don't know that, sir."

"Guess we'll find that out when we catch up to them, sir."

"Sergeant," McLain said, "you seem to be making a habit of telling me things I already know."

"I apologize, sir," Henderson said, even though given the chance he would rather have bitten off his tongue than do so. "I was just trying to be helpful."

"Well, I appreciate that, Sergeant, I really do," McLain said, "but save trying to be helpful for when I ask for help. All right?"

"As you say, sir."

"Guest?"

"Yes, sir?"

"I want to ride up ahead and locate those white men."

"Yes, sir."

"They may have seen something useful."

"Yes, sir."

"When you find them, come back and get us. I don't want you approaching them alone. Is that clear?"

"Clear, sir."

"Good," McLain said, "then get going."

"Sir?"

"Yes, Guest?"

"Are you plannin' to camp tonight?"

"Well . . . of course we are. We'll probably ride another hour or so, and then make camp. Don't stay out in the dark too long, Guest. If you don't locate the men tonight, you can do it tomorrow."

"Much obliged, Lieutenant," Guest said. He gave Henderson another look and said, "Save me some coffee and some grub."

"You'll have it," Henderson said.

"Go on, Guest!"

"I'm a-goin', Lieutenant," Guest said, wheeling his horse around. "I surely am."

TWENTY-TWO

Winston Guest wondered what he was doing still working for the Army. Invariably, he ended up riding with some young rooster like McLain, who spent most of his time puffing out his chest and flapping his feathers. Maybe it was time to get out and go back to the mountains.

It was dark, but he smelled something in the air that kept him from riding back to camp. He smelled coffee, and bacon. He knew that the coffee smell might be coming from the Army camp, except that the wind would be taking that odor the other way. Besides, he knew that they didn't have any bacon, just beans.

The smell of the bacon is what drew him. It made his mouth water, and even though he knew he wasn't going to get any, he wanted to see where the smell was coming from.

Finally he saw the light of a camp fire. He reined his horse in, dismounted, and left the animal there while he crept closer to take a look. When he got close enough he crouched down and surveyed the situation.

There were three white men in camp, drinking coffee and

eating bacon and some biscuits. His sharp eyes took everything in, including the fact that they had three horses, but four saddles. He didn't know many men to carry an extra saddle, so he assumed that they had come by this one dishonestly.

They looked like hard cases, all dressed similarly in trailworn clothes. The guns on their hips were not fancy, but they were functional. Most likely these were three desperados riding around looking for easy pickings. He wondered if they had seen any Indians about, but the young Lt. McLain had been right about one thing. It would be better for them all to ask that question together. Guest had no doubt that if he rode into that camp, he wouldn't be riding out, not without some bodies left behind and some lead in himself.

He turned and crept away back to his horse, mounted up and headed back to find the Army camp.

"Did you hear something?" Ben Fall asked, looking around.

"What are you so jumpy about?" Bunch asked. "Those soldiers probably camped a long time ago, and them Indians sure ain't gonna come up on us at night."

"What do you know about Indians?"

"I know they don't attack at night, I know that much," Bunch said.

"If you two are gonna keep up this bickering," Tucker Spring said, "I'm gonna make you pitch your own camps. Ben, what did you hear?"

"I don't know," Fall said. "Somethin'."

"I didn't hear—"

"Shut up, Earl," Spring said. "Let's just listen awhile."

All three men fell silent and listened intently.

"Do I hear a horse?" Fall asked.

"Maybe," Spring said, "just maybe you do."

"What do we do?" Fall asked.

"Nothin'," Spring said. "If it's anybody it's probably an Army scout."

"Then the Army will know where we are," Bunch said.

"We already figured to run into them tomorrow, Earl," Spring said, "so that's not a big surprise, is it?"

"Stupid," Fall said, under his breath.

"Just in case, though," Spring said, "Earl, you take the first watch, Ben you take the second and wake me up for mine."

"Right, Tuck."

"Now let's get some sleep. There's only one thing you two have got to remember for tomorrow."

"What's that?" Fall asked.

"When we do run into the soldiers," Spring said, "just let me do the talkin'."

TWENTY-THREE

The next morning Clint found himself outside, watching the Comanches break camp. He was surprised to see that it was the women who took the tipis down and, by the same token, would erect them again when they reached a new destination.

What he didn't know was that it took the women fifteen minutes to put up a tipi, and only five to take it back down again *and* pack it on horseback.

The tipis were made from tanned bison hides sewn together with the flesh side out, fitted over a framework of slender pine on cedar poles. They were always made in the same pattern, twenty-two poles to a frame, with a four pole base. Twenty bison skins fitted on over this frame, and when it was erected it formed a tipi twelve to fifteen feet in diameter.

Most of the men and male children were clad only in breechclout and moccasins. The women and female children were wearing buckskin dresses.

"We are ready to go," Tenawa came over to him and said.

"I'm impressed."

A young brave was watching them carefully, apparently waiting to talk to one of them.

"Who is this?" Clint asked Tenawa.

"That is Many Horses."

"Does he want to talk to me or you?"

"I do not know," she said, but she beckoned the brave to come closer. "What is it, Many Horses?"

"Have you seen Bold Wolf this morning, Tenawa?" the man asked.

"I have not."

"I haven't, either," Clint said, although he hadn't been asked.

The look the man gave him indicated that he hadn't been asked because Many Horses was not comfortable speaking to him.

"What is wrong?" Tenawa asked.

"No one has seen him."

"What did he say yesterday when Standing Stone told him about leaving?" Clint asked.

Now Many Horses had no choice but to speak to him, but he kept his eyes averted.

"He was angry. He did not say that he would be coming with us."

"He'll probably follow," Clint said. "If he doesn't, he'll be alone. I don't think he wants to be alone, do you, Many Horses?"

"Uh, no, no, I do not think so."

"He will follow," Tenawa said, touching the brave's arm. "We must go."

"Yes, all right," Many Horses said, and backed away. He seemed uncomfortable turning his back on Clint.

"They don't believe yet," Clint said, "but they're wary, aren't they?"

"Yes. No one will try anything, except perhaps Bold Wolf."

"He came to see me last night."

She looked at him.

"He did?"

He nodded.

"What did he say?"

"He threatened me," Clint said. "He told me to stay away from you, that you were his."

"I do not belong to him!" she said angrily.

"Well, that's kind of what I told him."

"What did you say . . . exactly?"

"I told him that I would stay away from you when you told me to."

"I will never do that."

"Well," Clint said, "he doesn't have to know that, now, does he?"

"He is dangerous, Clint, and you are not yet well enough to fight him."

"I'm hoping I don't have to fight him, Tenawa."

"The only way that will happen is if you make him believe that you are the Dreamwalker."

"Do you think there's a chance I can do that?" he asked.

She shook her head slowly and said, "I do not think there is any chance at all."

"Well, that's encouraging."

He looked around and saw that all of the women and children were lining up to walk. In fact, he did not see anyone on horseback.

"What's going on?" he asked.

"What do you mean?"

"No one is mounted."

"They have all said that if you are walking, they will walk, too."

"Even the young men?"

She nodded.

"Maybe there's more of a chance of making believers out of them than we thought."

"I think you can convince everyone—but Bold Wolf."

"Uh, Tenawa, what are the chances that Bold Wolf would do something . . . foolish?"

"Like what?"

"Would he, uh, try something from hiding?"

"Like a coward? I do not think so. When Bold Wolf fights you, it will be from right in front of you. He has much pride."

"Good," Clint said, "just so long as I see him coming."

TWENTY-FOUR

When they started off, Clint noticed that most of the young braves were carrying shields. Tenawa explained that these were horsehide war shields, with feathers and medicine symbols. The war shield was considered to have magical powers. Each warrior made his own war shield. It was painted with magical markings and the warrior decorated it with bear teeth, human hair, or horse tails, signifying that he was a great hunter, a deadly warrior . . . and a mighty horse thief.

"Horse thief?" Clint asked.

"Horses are power, remember?" Tenawa said. "It is considered a great feat if you can steal someone else's power."

These shields, she went on to explain, could deflect a lance or an arrow.

"What about a bullet?"

"Not at close range," she said, "but at the proper distance, yes."

Clint could understand that. The further a bullet had to travel, the less velocity it reached its target with.

"Have any of these shields been tested?" he asked.

"No," she said, "none of them."

"Well, let's hope they don't have to be."

Clint was leading Duke as he walked—or rather, Duke was following him. The others were leading their horses, but holding them for fear that they'd run off. Clint had no such fear with the big gelding.

"Tell me more about the shields," Clint said.

When not in use, she said, they were carried inside rawhide covers. Women—especially unclean women—were not permitted to touch them, for fear that their magic would be destroyed.

"Often," she finished, "they store their shields away from camp, so that no woman may come in contact with them."

"I guess there isn't much chance of there being any female warriors then, huh?"

"No," Tenawa said, laughing at the idea. "She could not get a shield that would protect her, could she?"

"No magic," he said.

"No magic," she repeated, and laughed.

It was decided that Clint and Duke would walk at the center of the column. Clint suspected he'd been given this position so that he could not lag behind and eventually ride away. Apparently, Standing Stone was still not completely sold on the idea of Clint as the Dreamwalker.

Likewise they probably didn't want him leading the column, either, lest he lead them into something.

Was Standing Stone suspicious of him in that respect at all? he wondered. He was impressed that not only Standing Stone but the other elderly members of the camp were walking. In reality, though, they didn't have that many horses, probably just enough for the young braves to ride. These people, he thought, must have incredible stamina to have gotten this far.

"What are you thinking?" Tenawa asked.

"That I am very much impressed by your people."

"You said that this morning," she said. "It makes you unlike most other white men."

"How many white men have you known, Tenawa?"

"Just the ones on the reservation. They are cruel. They treat my people badly and steal their food."

"Haven't your people complained about their treatment?" he asked.

"Complain to who?" she demanded. "The same people who mistreat them? There is no one to complain to."

"What of Quanah?"

"Quanah goes to Washington and poses for pictures," she said sadly.

Clint found that hard to believe. The Quanah he knew was a proud warrior, a proud man, and wouldn't pose for pictures for anyone.

"I can't believe that."

She looked at him, hearing something in his voice that interested her.

"Do you know Quanah?"

"I knew him once," Clint said. "A long time ago."

She gave him a different kind of look now, one of renewed respect.

"You knew Quanah?"

"Years ago, in the panhandle."

"Were you . . . friends?"

He thought about that for a moment, then said, "We could have been, I guess. We just never had much time to work on it."

"Have you told this to Standing Stone?"

"No, why?"

"Standing Stone has much respect for Quanah. He, too, knew him years ago when he was a different Quanah."

"Do you think that would mean more to him than my being the Dreamwalker?"

Now she thought a moment and said, "No. You would have to prove that to him, too."

"I don't know how I could prove to him that I knew Quanah," Clint said, "unless Quanah had already talked to him about me."

"I . . . don't know."

"What if he did?" Clint said thoughtfully.

"What do you mean?"

"What if Standing Stone already knows who I am because he heard about me from Quanah?"

"Why would he recognize you?"

"Well, I haven't changed all that much since then," Clint said, "but I'm sure Quanah would have described Duke to your father."

"But if my father knows who you are," she asked, "why wouldn't he say so?"

"That's what I'd like to know."

TWENTY-FIVE

When Winston Guest returned to the Army camp the night before and told Lt. McLain about the three men he had seen, the lieutenant said, "We'll visit those fellas first thing in the morning."

It wasn't even first light when Guest was shaken awake by Henderson.

"McLain wants to reach that camp you saw before they can start moving again."

Guest frowned and asked, "What if they got up even earlier than we did?"

Henderson looked at the sky and said, "Nobody got up earlier than we did."

Guest got up, grabbed a quick cup of coffee, and then saddled his horse, a big Appaloosa he'd had for several years. This horse was the fastest thing he'd ever ridden, and certainly the fastest animal in the Army. He'd won several races proving that.

"Take the point, Mr. Guest," Lt. McLain said. The young man looked well rested and impeccable while everyone else looked tired and bedraggled. Guest wished he knew how the man did it. "Show us where that camp is."

"Yes, sir."

"Wake up," Tucker Spring said, kicking first Earl Bunch and then Ben Fall in the side. "They're comin'."

"Huh?" Bunch said.

"Who's comin'?" Fall asked.

"The soldiers."

Fall got quickly to his feet and strapped his gun on.

"If you draw that gun at any time," Spring said, "I'll kill you myself."

"What?"

"Just relax and let me do the talkin'," Spring said. "That goes for both of you."

Bunch staggered to his feet, still more asleep than awake.

"Earl, you understand?"

"Huh? Sure, Tuck, sure, I understand."

"Ben?"

"Yeah, yeah . . ."

For a small man Ben Fall had a huge temper. Spring only hoped it wouldn't get them killed.

When the soldiers came into view of the camp, all three men were dressed, standing, and armed.

"Whoa!" McLain said, halting his column. "Mr. Guest, Sergeant Henderson, you are with me. The rest of you stay here and wait. Corporal?"

Corporal Will Elmer came riding up next to the young lieutenant. Elmer had even more time in the Army than Sergeant Henderson. It had never bothered him to have to take orders from the young officers West Point was constantly spitting out, but it galled him to have to take orders from this one.

"Yes, sir?"

"At first sign of trouble you will bring the men in with you, guns drawn."

"Yes, sir."

McLain looked at Guest and Henderson and in a heavy Boston accent said, "Gentlemen."

He started forward, and Guest and Henderson followed first, then flanked him.

"Remember what I said," Spring said out of the side of his mouth. "I do the talking."

"Yeah, yeah," Fall said.

Bunch was already remaining silent.

Spring liked the idea that only three men were approaching them. If push came to shove they could kill these three and then take cover against the rest. He, Bunch, and Fall would end up dead eventually, he knew that, but they'd take a bunch of blue bellies with them.

"Hello the camp," McLain called, as if they hadn't been seen approaching.

"Hello, Lieutenant," Spring said. "Sorry we don't have any coffee to offer you. We weren't expecting any company this mornin'."

"That's all right, sir. My name is Lieutenant Kenneth McLain, Fourth Cavalry. This is Sergeant Henderson, and that is my scout, Winston Guest."

Spring looked at Guest.

"I've heard of you."

Guest did not reply.

"And your names?"

"My name's Tucker Spring," Spring said, "these fellas are Mr. Bunch and Mr. Fall."

Fall was wanted in New Mexico, Bunch was wanted in Utah. Spring was wanted in a couple of southern states. He had fought for the Confederacy as a young man and was not very happy with the outcome to this day.

"Mr. Spring, we are looking for some Comanches who have, uh, drifted away from the reservation. Have you seen any Indians?"

"I haven't," Spring said, "but one of my associates has.

Mr. Bunch, here, said he saw some Indians just yesterday af-
ternoon.''

"Did he?" McLain said. He looked at Bunch and asked,
"Were they Comanches?"

Bunch didn't answer.

"Answer the man, Mr. Bunch," Spring said.

"But you said—"

"I'm suggesting now that you answer the lieutenant. He's
a very busy man."

Bunch, confused, looked up at McLain and said, ''I
dunno.''

"Sir?"

"I don't know if they was Comanches. I don't know Indians
that well."

"Could you describe them?"

"Not well," Bunch said. "I seen them from a distance.
'Bout five of them was up in some rocks."

"Could you tell Mr. Guest here where those rocks are so
that we may go and take a look?"

"I guess so."

Bunch took a minute or two to try to describe the area to
Guest.

"I can find it," he told McLain.

"We're obliged to you for your help, sir," McLain said to
Spring.

"Our pleasure, Lieutenant."

"Do I detect some Southern in your accent, Mr. Spring?"
McLain asked.

"You do, sir. I'm from Alabama."

"Served in the war, did you?"

"I had that honor."

"I'm afraid I was, uh, too young to make it, myself."

"You were lucky, sir."

"Was I? Do you think so?"

"Yes, sir."

If you were in the war, Spring thought, you posturing blue
belly, you'd be dead by now.

"Very well," McLain said, "then our business here is done."

"I'd like to ask a question, Lieutenant," Guest said. "I see you've got an extra saddle—"

"That's enough, Mr. Guest," McLain said, cutting him off. "We have work to do."

Spring had tensed when Guest mentioned the extra saddle. The man had good eyes, and was smart.

"I just want to ask about that extra—"

"Mr. Guest! We are through here. Gentlemen," he said, to Spring, Bunch, and Fall, "thank you."

"Our pleasure to help, Lieutenant."

McLain turned his horse in Guest's direction so that the scout had no choice but to turn his as well.

Spring watched the three men ride back to the soldiers, then watched them all ride off.

TWENTY-SIX

"I thought you said you was gonna do all the talking," Bunch whined.

"Shut up."

"That scout was interested in the extra saddle," Fall said.

"I know."

"Why?"

"Because he's smart, that's why. He took one look at us and knew what we were."

"What do we do now?" Fall asked.

"We get movin'," Spring said, "before they decide to come back."

Winston Guest was furious with McLain for not letting him ask about the extra saddle. McLain seemed oblivious to the possibility that the three men might have killed somebody for it. When Guest pointed it out to the man as they rode away, his reaction was even more infuriating.

"Our mission out here is to retrieve those Indians, Mr. Guest."

"I know that, Lieutenant, but if we happen to discover a crime committed by white men against white men—"

"Not our job," McLain said. "There are territorial authorities for that sort of thing."

"Lieutenant—"

"If you like, Mr. Guest, you may bring your suspicions to the attention of the proper authorities, if and when we come across them."

"Lieutenant—"

"That's all I want to hear on the subject, Mr. Guest. Please be so kind as to do your job now and find me the rocks those men said they saw some Indians on."

"Did it occur to you, Lieutenant, that they might be lying?"

"Why would they lie?"

"To send us south," Guest said, "the opposite direction from which they are traveling."

"Nonsense," McLain said, "they had no time to prepare such a lie. Move on ahead, Mr. Guest."

Guest looked at Sergeant Henderson, who gave him a helpless shrug.

"Yes, sir," Guest said, and rode on ahead, if just to get away from the man.

"You think they'll be back?" Bunch asked Spring as the three men prepared to mount up.

"Not if they find those Indians," Spring said.

"That is, if Earl really did see any Indians," Ben Fall pointed out.

"I saw some Indians, Ben," Bunch said, with feeling.

"So you say."

"Tuck, don't you think I saw some Indians?"

"I don't know what you saw," Spring said, mounting up, "but I hope it was some Indians, and I hope there are more where they came from."

"Why?" Bunch asked.

"To keep those soldiers busy, that's why," Ben Fall said.

"Oh."

"Come on," Spring said, "mount up."

Fall and Bunch climbed atop their horses and they started on their way.

"Was that true, what you told that soldier, Tuck?" Bunch asked.

"About what?"

"About fighting in the war."

"It was true."

"You must have been real young."

"I was."

"Bet you killed lots of Union soldiers, huh?" Bunch asked.

"Not enough," Spring said, "not nearly enough."

TWENTY-SEVEN

It quickly became clear to Clint that Comanches did not rest. They continued on—walking or riding—until they either reached their destination, or until night fell.

Clint, in his weakened condition, did not have that much stamina.

"Tenawa, I have to stop," he said.

He saw that she looked worried. She probably wondered what the others would say—especially the young men—if he could not even keep pace with the elders.

"Don't worry," Clint said. "You can tell them that while the Dreamwalker is in the body of a man, he is limited by that body. Since my body is injured, it must rest."

"All right."

Abruptly, Clint stopped, and those Indians walking behind his stopped as well. Standing Stone and Many Horses were walking up ahead, and Tenawa ran to tell them what Clint had said. She returned with both men to where Clint was sitting on a rock.

"Are you well?" Standing Stone asked.

"Well enough," Clint said, "but tired. I just need to stop for a short time."

"Very well," Standing Stone said. "We will take a short rest."

The old man walked off and was joined by the younger ones, who were obviously questioning his decision to stop.

"Should I go over and talk to them?" Tenawa asked.

"Let your father handle it, Tenawa," Clint said. "He'll know what to say. If you hear some grumbling from others, though, you can repeat what I told you."

"Very well."

Clint became aware that most of the others were watching him closely, obviously wondering why they had stopped.

While he was seated Tenawa took the opportunity to check his wounds.

"Am I bleeding?" he asked.

"No."

"Good."

"But you should rest longer."

"Just a few minutes," he said.

Standing Stone and Many Horses came walking back over to speak to him.

"We have decided," Standing Stone said, "that you should ride."

"I can walk—"

"If you walk," Standing Stone said, "because you were injured you will have to stop many times to rest. If you ride, we will make better time."

"What about the others?"

"They will walk."

"We should send someone back on horseback to see if there's anyone behind us."

"Someone is already doing that," Standing Stone said.

"Who?"

"Bold Wolf. He has been behind us the whole time."

That figured. He didn't want to ride with them, so he rode behind them. Clint gave the young brave credit for doing that, covering their rear, rather than riding up ahead of them.

"All right," Clint said, finally giving in.

"You will ride the Black Stallion."

Standing Stone's words were heard and Clint heard several sharp intakes of breath.

"If he is the Dreamwalker," Many Horses said, "he and the Black Stallion could fly away."

"If he does that," Standing Stone said, "then so be it."

The old man looked around to see if anyone else objected. No one said anything.

"Many Horses," Standing Stone said then, "you and Little Buffalo help him up onto the Black Stallion."

"Should we throw a blanket on the Black Stallion?" Little Buffalo asked.

"No need," Clint said, "I will ride bareback."

Many Horses and Little Buffalo boosted Clint up onto Duke's back, while the big, black gelding stood motionless. The maneuver pulled on his wounds a bit, but he didn't think it started any of them bleeding again.

"Okay, big boy," he said, patting Duke's neck and whispering in his ear, "we're just going to walk awhile, just walk."

He could feel the gelding's muscles bunching underneath his thighs. Duke wanted to run, but Clint wasn't ready for that yet. Riding Duke at full gallop would surely cause his wounds to open, and there was no need for it. He was not in any real danger at the present time.

While he was astride Duke someone handed him a water pouch. He took one swallow and handed it back. He noticed that no one else was taking water.

Some Dreamwalker, he thought.

Bold Wolf saw the People stop ahead of him, and he stopped as well. So far he had seen no one coming behind them, but if they stopped like this again they were not going to make good time.

He watched with sharp eyes and saw them boost the white

man up onto the black horse. He shook his head, but at least this would keep them moving.

Wouldn't this prove to everyone, though, that the white man was not the Dreamwalker?

TWENTY-EIGHT

Winston Guest crouched and studied the ground. There had indeed been horses on these rocks and not shod horses. Apparently that hard case had been telling the truth, at least about seeing some Indians.

He was still angry with McLain for not allowing him to question Spring and his men about the extra saddle. There was no doubt that Spring was the leader of the three, and Guest had also noticed the man's Southern accent. It must have galled the man to have to answer questions put to him by a "blue belly"—and one who was an idiot, at that.

Guest stood up and looked around. The tracks were faint but he could follow them. Most likely this had been a scouting party for the renegade Comanches. He had little doubt the tracks would lead him to their camp.

Sometime later Winston Guest found where the Comanches had been camped. There were plenty of cold fires, including those that had been built inside of the tipis. From the appearance of the site, they had camped here long enough for their tracks leading here to have been wiped out by time and weather. Only the scouting party's tracks remained. Their tracks leading away from here, however, were sharp and clear—so clear that he could make out the tracks of a single shod horse. Either they'd stolen a horse from some white man, or there was a white man traveling with them.

The tracks were easily followed, heading northwest. He stood there for a moment, wondering whether he should follow them himself, or ride back to McLain and the others. He decided in the end to follow the tracks himself. His decision was motivated in part by the desire to postpone seeing Lt. Kenneth McLain again for as long as possible.

Guest mounted his horse and started following the tracks.

"Guest should have been back by now," McLain said, frowning.

"He'll be back, Lieutenant," Sergeant Henderson said.

"He should have been back by now," McLain said again. "How are we supposed to—which way—"

Henderson realized then that McLain was afraid. Without Winston Guest to direct them, the lieutenant would be totally lost. This was a revelation for the sergeant. It made the man seem so much more human.

"We'll just keep going northwest, Lieutenant," Henderson said. "We'll meet up with him somewhere along the line."

"He's only supposed to find a trail and then come back for us," McLain said. "What if he's following the trail himself?"

"Lieutenant, I don't think Guest is going to try to bring all those Comanches in by himself. When he finds them he'll be back for us. Meanwhile, I suggest that we just keep on moving."

McLain turned to Henderson, and the officer looked very young to the sergeant at that moment. His eyes were watery and lost-looking, but he firmed his jaw and said, "Very well, Sergeant. Your suggestion is a sound one."

"Thank you, sir."

"Get the men ready to roll."

"Yes, sir."

Henderson went back and spoke with Corporal Elmer.

"Sounds like the young lieutenant is about to fall apart," Elmer said.

"I didn't have any idea," Henderson said. "He puts up a good front, but he's so scared that Winston won't come back."

"Does he think Guest is the only one who knows where he is?"

"I think Guest is the horse he's hitched his wagon to," Henderson said.

"What do you make of Guest?"

"He hates bein' around McLain," Henderson said. "He ain't gonna come back until he absolutely has to."

"That means if he finds a trail he's gonna follow it," Elmer said.

"I think so."

"Sergeant!" McLain called.

"You better get the men ready to go, Corporal," Henderson said.

"Yes, sir," Elmer said.

Henderson went back to the head of the column with McLain. He decided he had better stay right at the young lieutenant's side.

TWENTY-NINE

They stopped traveling just before dark, for which Clint was grateful. Even though he'd been riding on Duke's back, the day had taken its toll on him. Many Horses and Running Antelope helped him down from the horse and he immediately sat down on the ground. He watched while they built fires and pitched camp without erecting any of the tipis. They wouldn't do that until they found a place where they were going to stay for a while.

There was a lot of activity around him, and he was amazed as he watched at how efficient everyone was. Even the children were given jobs to do, and they did them quickly. Before long several fires were going and he could smell food cooking.

Tenawa came over and sat down with him.

"How do you feel?"

"Tired, but okay."

"I will have someone prepare a bed for you," she said. "You need your rest."

"Not for a while. I want to sit and look around."

"They are looking at you, too."

"I know."

"The children are very curious about you, ever since you let them take a close look at . . . Duke?"

"Yes, Duke," Clint said. "I think he prefers being called that than 'the Black Stallion.' "

"And you would like to be called Clint and not the Dreamwalker?"

"That depends on what's going to keep me alive."

"I do not think you are in any danger anymore," she said. "In fact, if you wanted to leave I don't think anyone would stop you."

"What about Standing Stone?"

"I don't think so."

"And Bold Wolf?"

"I am not so sure about him."

"Well, I don't think I'll be leaving for a while. I'm not in shape to be on my own yet, and when I'm not afraid for my life this is not a bad place to be."

At that moment they heard a horse approaching.

"It is Bold Wolf!" someone shouted.

The young brave rode into camp and dismounted before the pony came to a stop. He looked around, saw Standing Stone and Many Horses and walked over to them.

"Quick," Clint said, "go and find out what he's got to say."

Tenawa nodded and ran over to join the men. Clint wondered if they'd shoo her away, but they did not. She listened intently as Bold Wolf did most of the talking and then hurried back to Clint.

"He says there is no sign that we are being followed."

"How far back?"

"He says a full day."

That meant Bold Wolf had been doing some hard riding to know that they were a day clear of anyone coming behind them.

"What else did he have to say?"

"That we were moving too slowly."

"And I'll bet he blames me."

"Yes."

"Well, fine," Clint said. "I'm willing to stay right here until I'm well enough to ride, and the rest of you can get going tomorrow."

"I will not leave you," she said, "but I will mention that to my father."

"I don't think Bold Wolf would agree."

"Maybe he would," she said. "It would keep you and me apart."

"You have a point there. Did he have anything else to say?"

"Yes," she said. "He's hungry."

They were all hungry and as soon as the food was prepared Tenawa brought a wooden bowl over to Clint and then sat next to him with one of her own. As always he didn't bother to ask what they were eating.

The more he thought about it, the more Clint wished that the Comanches would leave him behind and go on by themselves. It wasn't that he wanted to escape from them anymore, he just wanted them to be safe. The question was, would they believe that was his motive?

"Tell me something," Clint said to Tenawa.

"What?"

"Does it really matter now if I can prove that I'm the Dreamwalker?"

"To Standing Stone?"

"To anyone."

She thought a moment.

"The children, they already think you are. The women, I don't think they care. The young men, I'm not sure they believe. The old men . . . they might be the only ones you have to convince."

"How many old men are there, besides your father?"

"Only a few."

"Is Bold Wolf actually the leader?"

"It is a combination," she said, "of Bold Wolf's youth and strength with the wisdom of the old ones."

"When it comes right down to it," Clint said, "who will the others follow, Standing Stone or Bold Wolf?"

"Standing Stone, I think," she said, "unless . . ."

"Unless what?"

"Unless Bold Wolf can convince them that you are a spy."

"For who?"

"The Army."

"You mean he thinks I'm an advance scout for the Army or something?"

"That is what he said when he rode in before."

"If he gets anyone to believe that, my life could be in danger all over again."

"Yes."

"And I'm stuck once again with proving that I'm the Dreamwalker."

"Yes."

"I'm back where I started."

She didn't reply.

"Not much chance of getting them to leave me behind, then, is there?"

"That depends on Standing Stone," she said. "If you can convince him there might be a chance."

Clint fell silent for a while, finishing his meal and trying to decide what to do next. As far as his life being in danger, that seemed to be the case only when Bold Wolf was entered into the mix. He thought he should probably concern himself with that rather than with the Comanches staying off the reservation. Truth be told, if it wasn't for Tenawa being with them he wouldn't be so concerned about that. The longer they stayed off the reservation the more chance there was that they'd kill somebody—or end up getting killed themselves.

"Do you want more food?"

"No," Clint said, handing her the bowl. "Do me a favor, Tenawa."

"Yes?"

"Tell Standing Stone I want to talk to him."

"All right."

"And tell him I want to talk to him now!"

THIRTY

Clint knew he was pushing his luck again, but he didn't see that he had much choice. He had to convince Standing Stone to do as he said and leave him behind—and even if he did, he still might have to deal with Bold Wolf. With everyone thinking that he might be the Dreamwalker, Bold Wolf would gain that much more respect if he exposed him—or killed him.

That reminded him of something else he had to ask Tenawa. When she returned she looked grim.

"Well?"

"I told him."

"And?"

"He is angry."

"And?"

"And he is coming over to talk to you." She seemed surprised by this.

"Okay, before he gets here tell me what I had when your men found me."

"Nothing."

"Nothing? No weapons at all?"

"None."

Damn it. The three men who had robbed him took his guns. Now he had to get away from the Comanches alive so he could hunt them down and get back his guns, not to mention his saddle.

"Do your people have any guns, Tenawa?"

"Some of our men have rifles."

"No handguns?"

She hesitated, then said, "One."

"Who has it?"

"Bold Wolf."

He would have preferred that someone else have that particular item, but at least he had a chance to get his hands on a weapon.

He was about to ask her further questions when he saw Standing Stone approaching them. The shaman's steps were ponderous and his face was set even firmer than usual.

"I think you better let me talk to your father alone, Tenawa."

"Yes."

She stood up and waited for her father to reach them.

"You wanted to talk?" he asked.

"Yes."

The shaman looked at his daughter, who bobbed her head and left, walking away quickly.

"You dare to summon me this way?" Standing Stone demanded.

"Don't get excited," Clint said. "Sit down. We need to talk."

Standing Stone stared at him a few moments, then sat next to him.

"Standing Stone, you and I both know that I'm not the Dreamwalker."

The man didn't answer.

"I think you wanted me to be for the sake of your people."

"Why would I want that?"

"Well, I've given that some thought. At first I thought you

simply wanted me to give your people some hope for a good life.''

"And you no longer think that?''

"No, I don't. I think you want me to convince your people to go back to the reservation.''

The old man stared at him, and then looked away.

"Am I close? I think you're sorry you left the reservation. In fact, I'd even bet you only went along so that you could persuade them at some point to go back.''

There was no reply.

"I think you only want to keep your people alive, Standing Stone. I commend you for that. When you saw how they reacted to my horse, you convinced them that he was the Black Stallion. That made me the Dreamwalker.''

Standing Stone was still looking away.

"How close am I, Standing Stone?''

The old man hesitated, then looked at Clint and said, "You are not close, you are right.''

"You don't believe in the legend of the Dreamwalker, then?''

"I do not believe that you are the Dreamwalker.''

"But you do believe in it.''

"Yes.''

"And the others?''

"Many of them believe.''

"And many do not.''

"Yes.''

"And Bold Wolf?''

"He is young,'' Standing Stone said. "He believes in very little that he cannot touch.''

"And the others? Many Horses? Little Buffalo? Running Antelope? What do they believe in?''

"I do not know.''

"I think they believe in you, and in Bold Wolf. I think they'd follow either one of you.''

"Perhaps.''

"What do you want, most of all, Standing Stone?''

"It is as you said," the old man answered. "I want my people to live."

"On the reservation?"

"Living on the reservation is harsh," he said, "but out here they will end up killed. Young soldiers will come, and the young braves will fight, and we will all be wiped out. That is the way it will be."

"How do you expect to get them back to the reservation?"

"I did not see a way, until you came along."

"You think if they believed that I was the Dreamwalker they would do what I said?"

"Yes."

"Well, I think we have a better chance of convincing them, working together, than I had of convincing you, don't you think?"

"Yes, I do."

THIRTY-ONE

Clint told Standing Stone how he felt about things. The Comanches would make better time without him, but as it turned out, Standing Stone didn't care. If they made good time it would be that much further to go back to the reservation. That was why he made them camp for so long. Finding Clint and nursing him back to help as the possible Dreamwalker added to that time.

"Then we have to convince them to turn back," Clint said.

"How?"

"Have you tried?"

"Not yet," Standing Stone said. "I have been waiting for the right time."

"Then perhaps this is it."

"Perhaps."

"It seems to me that the young braves are the ones who have to be convinced," Clint said. "The others—the older ones, the women, the children—will probably go along."

"That is as I see it."

"And the hardest of the young braves to convince will naturally be Bold Wolf."

"Yes."

"Then I think we should convince the others first," Clint said, "and leave him for last."

"How do we do that?"

"It will take some thought," Clint said. "What you and I have to decide, Standing Stone, is what our relationship is. I understand that Bold Wolf has suggested that I might be an Army spy."

"Yes."

"Do you believe that?"

"No."

"Why not?"

"You do not strike me as the Army type."

Clint laughed.

"I'm not. Also, I have to understand whether or not I should fear for my safety from you and your people."

"You have nothing to fear from me," the shaman said, "or from most of my people."

"Again, we're talking about Bold Wolf."

"Yes."

"So as far as you're concerned, I could ride out of here in the morning on my own."

"You could," Standing Stone said, "but you would not last very long."

"I know," Clint said, wincing at the thought of spending a couple of days on horseback.

"So you will stay with us?"

"I will stay until I am well," Clint said, "and until we have convinced your people to go back."

"Why?"

"Why what?"

"Why should you care if we go back or not?"

"I'm concerned about Tenawa."

Standing Stone stared at him.

"I like her, and I would not like to see her get hurt."

"Do you want to marry my daughter?"

"I've only known her a short time, Standing Stone. I don't

know how it works among your people, but among mine two people have to know each other awhile before they decide to get married.''

''She wants to marry you.''

''Has she said so?''

The old man shook his head.

''She does not have to. I see how she looks at you, the look in her eyes when she talks about you.''

''I understand she is to marry Bold Wolf.''

''He wants to marry her,'' Standing Stone said. ''That is not the same as getting married.''

''Can we put aside the question of who is going to marry who for a later time?'' Clint asked hopefully. ''We have other problems to address.''

''Yes, you are right.''

Clint looked out at the others and saw Bold Wolf watching him and Standing Stone. The look on the young brave's face was one of pure hatred.

Bold Wolf, he thought, would not be an easy obstacle to get around.

THIRTY-TWO

Later, Tenawa came to him. Shyly at first, standing tentatively.

He grabbed her wrist and pulled her down so that she was sitting next to him.

"Listen . . ." he said, and told her what he and Standing Stone were planning.

She seemed more surprised that her father never believed that he was the Dreamwalker.

"He fooled me," she said.

"Well, let's hope that both he and I can fool everyone else," Clint said.

"I did not even know that he wanted us to go back," she said, shaking her head.

"He wants to save lives, Tenawa, that's his only motive."

"I thought he hated the reservation."

"He does, but he thinks it's better than having everyone die out here."

"Why does he think we'll die?"

"Young men," Clint said. "He's worried about how Bold

Wolf and the other young braves will react when the soldiers catch up, and he knows that the soldiers will be young men. He's worried about how they will react to Bold Wolf and the others. Caught in the cross fire will be everyone else.''

She listened intently, nodding with understanding.

"If it wasn't for Bold Wolf," Clint said, "I think he might have just come out and told everyone to go back."

"Oh, they would not," she said. "Many Horses, Little Buffalo, and the others are not as headstrong as Bold Wolf, but they do not want to go back."

"Unless the Dreamwalker tells them to," Clint said.

"Perhaps."

"You'll have to help, Tenawa."

"I will do whatever I can," she promised.

"Good. With you, and me and your father working together I think we'll be able to turn them and get them to go back."

"Not Bold Wolf," she said. "He will never go back."

"Well, if we get most of them to go back . . ." he said, letting it trail off.

"The women and, of course, the children will follow Standing Stone. So will the old ones. The young men . . . they still might follow Bold Wolf."

"We'll have to see what happens."

"When will we do this?"

"Not for a few days," Clint said. "We want to find another good campsite. Once everyone is settled in we'll put our plan into effect."

"What *is* the plan?" she asked.

Sheepishly he said, "Well, we don't quite have that worked out yet."

"When will you?" she asked.

"Oh, by the time we camp I'm sure Standing Stone and I will have worked it out," he said, patting her hand. "Don't worry."

He said it with more confidence than he felt.

THIRTY-THREE

Guest rode into the Army camp late again. He was hoping that McLain would be asleep, but he wasn't. He was in his tent, with a lamp burning, so that all of his men could see his silhouette.

Guest dismounted and handed his horse over to a private. He turned and saw Henderson approaching him, carrying a cup of coffee.

"Here," the sergeant said, "you look like you could use this."

"Thanks," Guest said. He sipped the coffee and looked over at the command tent. "Why does he insist on using that thing?"

"I don't know," Henderson said. "I guess it makes him feel like General Grant on the battlefield."

"If he ever makes general we'll all be in trouble."

"He will, don't worry," Henderson said, "and we will. What did you find?"

"A trail. I followed it for a while, but I think we're a little more than a day behind."

"They've got women and children," the other man said. "We'll catch up to them."

"There was never any doubt of that," Guest said. "I'm just worried about these young soldiers of yours."

"I know," Henderson said. "They're liable to be a little trigger-happy, and there are young braves on the other side."

"A formula for disaster," Guest said, sipping coffee again. "I'd like to find them myself, maybe with you and Will Elmer. We'd keep our heads."

"You got that right."

Guest finished his coffee and handed the cup back after scattering the remnants on the ground.

"Guess I better check in."

"There's something I should tell you."

"What?"

Henderson told Guest what he thought he'd figured out about McLain.

"Well, hell, man," Guest said, "anyone could see the man's scared all the time."

Henderson looked surprised.

"Well, he had me fooled."

"That's because he's your superior officer," Guest said. "You don't look at him the way I do."

"He's your superior, too."

"No," Guest said. "You're in the Army, I'm just employed by it. He's not my superior. Any grub left?"

"We saved you some."

"I'll be right out."

Henderson watched Guest walk to the command tent, then turned and walked back to one of the camp fires.

As Guest entered the tent, Lieutenant McLain looked up from his field table. Another affectation for a man who felt he was born too late. The scout saw the man's relief clearly on his face before he could cover it.

"Ah, Guest, you're back," McLain said, as casually as he could. "Did you find our Comanches?"

"Found a trail, Lieutenant. We're about a day behind them, maybe a little more. We should catch up to them in two days, at the most."

"Good. These renegades have been out on their own too long."

"They're not renegades, Lieutenant," Guest said. "They're mostly women, children, and old men."

"If they're not on the reservation," McLain said officiously, "they're renegades."

"It's that kind of attitude that is gonna get some people killed when we do catch up to them."

"That will be their choice."

"No, sir," Guest said, "the choice is ours."

"What are you saying, Mr. Guest?"

"Lieutenant, I'm requestin' that you give me Henderson and Elmer and let us go and find those Comanches. The three of us can catch up to them in no time and convince them to come back."

"And what do you suggest the rest of us do in the meantime?" McLain asked.

"Stay back and shine your sabers."

"Guest," McLain said, "I'm sensing an attitude here."

"Let me make it real clear, then . . . sir," Guest said. "With the attitude you're showin', some of your young soldiers out there are gonna be pretty quick on the trigger when we catch up to the Comanches. This is not a war party we're trailin', it's a bunch of reservation Indians."

"There are at least a dozen young braves with them, Mr. Guest. Must I remind you of that?"

"All of whom grew up on the reservation," Guest said. "They have no more experience than your soldiers. We're gonna have young men on both sides thinkin' they got somethin' to prove."

"What are you suggesting, Mr. Guest?"

Guest stared at the young officer as if he were stupid, because he sure was *acting* stupid.

"I'm not suggestin' anything, Lieutenant," he said. "I'm

tellin' you, based on my experience, that we have a dangerous situation here. If you go ridin' up on those Indians in force, they're gonna fight.''

"My men are ready.''

"Are you deliberately bein' dense?'' Guest asked before he could stop himself.

"Mr. Guest!'' McLain said, standing up quickly, back ramrod straight. "You are addressin' an officer in the United States Army.''

"I'm addressin' a damned fool, if you ask me,'' Guest said. He figured he might as well go all the way.

"You're an inch away from a court-martial,'' McLain said. "Or I could have you shot right here on the battlefield—''

"What battlefield?'' Guest asked, cutting the man off. "Son, listen to me closely. We ain't on a battlefield. There's no war. Just some Indians who got tired of white Indian agents stealin' their food.''

"If there was thievery going on they should have reported it.''

"Right,'' Guest said, "to the agents who were stealin' it.''

"Mr. Guest, am I to understand that your sympathies are with the enemy?''

Winston Guest wanted nothing more than to reach across the table and slap some sense into the young lieutenant. He knew if he did that, though, he just *might* get shot.

"Lieutenant,'' Guest said, "you can understand anythin' you like. I'm through talkin', because you ain't hearin' a word I say.''

Guest turned and left, and Lieutenant Kenneth McLain stared after him in total confusion. There had been no class in this at West Point.

THIRTY-FOUR

At first light the next day Lieutenant McLain was informed by Private Jeff Morgan that Sergeant Henderson, Corporal Elmer, and Mr. Guest were not in camp.

"Where did they go?" he demanded.

"They left before first light, sir."

Panic welled up inside McLain, and he fought to push it down.

"What are we supposed to do?" he said aloud.

"Sir?" the private asked. "I thought you were supposed to tell us that."

At first light Ben Fall shook Tucker Spring awake.

"Bad news."

"What?" Spring asked, annoyed.

"Your horse must have stepped on a stone yesterday," Fall said. "His front right is too sore for him to put weight on."

"Christ." Spring rubbed his hand over his face.

"What do we do?" Fall asked.

"We can't stay here," Spring said. "There's a town west of here, called Rock Springs."

"How long will it take us to walk it?"

"We ain't gonna walk it," Spring said, getting to his feet.

"We got to if we're gonna take your horse."

"We're not takin' my horse. I'll ride double with one of you and we'll make Rock Springs by noon."

"And then what?"

"And then I'll buy another horse."

"What about this horse? Do we shoot it?"

"No, we don't shoot it. Just let it go. It'll heal on its own and be fine."

He looked around and saw that there wasn't a coffeepot on the fire.

"Jesus Christ," he said, "I've got to make the coffee, too? What the hell good are you?"

"Clint?"

He looked up at Tenawa.

"It's time."

He sat up and looked around. He was annoyed to find that almost everyone was ready to continue and he had slept through their preparations. He must have been even more exhausted than he thought.

"I'm ready," he said.

He struggled to his feet, and it seemed that every muscle in his body ached. His back was stiff, and Tenawa took the time to check his wounds.

"No bleeding," she said. "That is good."

"That's excellent," he said, "but it still feels stiff."

He looked around and saw Standing Stone, Many Horses, Running Antelope, and many of the others. He did not see Bold Wolf.

"Bold Wolf rode out earlier," Tenawa said, as if reading his mind.

"Ahead or behind?" Clint said.

"Behind."

The man may have been headstrong but apparently he had some smarts.

"Are you all right?" she asked.

"I'm fine." He tried to stretch without hurting his back, but was unsuccessful. "It's just too bad you don't know how to make coffee."

"I do," she said. "I learned in school."

"Great."

"But we do not have any."

"Great," he said, with a lot less enthusiasm.

THIRTY-FIVE

"We're gonna get court-martialed," Corporal Will Elmer said.

"That's the fifth time you've said that since we left camp," Sergeant Henderson said. "You didn't have to come with us, you know."

"I know."

"You can always go back, you know."

"I know."

"You don't want to go back, Will," Winston Guest said.

"I don't?"

"No, you'd just have to explain what happened to McLain and then take some more of his stupid orders. Stay with us, Corporal."

"Sure," Elmer said. "My career in the Army is over, anyway. We're gonna get court-martialed."

"Stop talking and let's ride," Guest said. "Judging by their tracks, they're walking. Riding hard we could probably catch up to them by early evening."

"They might have somebody watching their back trail," Henderson said.

"They probably will," Guest said, "but let's deal with that problem when we come to it."

It was a little after noon when Tucker Spring, Ben Fall, and Earl Bunch rode into Rock Springs. Spring was riding double behind Fall, and by the time they reached town it seemed likely they were going to need two new horses.

"We're gonna spend money on two horses?" Fall complained.

"Not necessarily," Spring said. "I've got an idea."

"What?"

"Let's talk about it after we leave these two horses at the livery."

They rode to the livery and dismounted. A old-timer came out and gave their horses the once-over.

"This one's about to fall down," he said, indicating the horse they had ridden double on.

Spring dropped his saddle on the ground and said, "Mine already did. We had no choice but to ride double."

"Well, this one's gonna need lots of rest, and even then he may be done in."

"You got horses for sale?" Spring asked.

"Got some."

"Well, then, I guess we'll be talkin' to you later today or tomorrow."

"I'll be here."

"Then just keep these two for us for now—and my saddle if you don't mind."

"I don't mind," the man said, "long as you're willin' to pay."

"We'll pay."

The man agreed to let them pay later. It was the kind of trust men like Tucker Spring lived for, and took advantage of.

As the three of them walked away from the livery, Fall asked, "What's your idea?"

"Let's take a look around this town and see what kind of law they've got," Spring said.

Fall thought he understood.

"We're gonna steal the horses, ain't we?"

"Well, for a start," Spring said.

"Whataya mean, a start?" Bunch asked.

"Rock Springs ain't a big town, but it ain't a small one either," Spring said.

"What's that got to do with anything?" Bunch asked, confused.

"A town this size," Spring said, "it's got to have a bank."

THIRTY-SIX

Clint was getting through this day a lot easier than the day before. He hadn't walked at all today, but had ridden Duke right from morning. Even though the Comanches did not stop to rest, he wasn't feeling all that worn-out. He knew, though, that when he dismounted he'd feel it in his butt, and his bones. Riding bareback was not something that he was used to.

At one point, about midday, he realized that he knew where he was. If he wasn't mistaken, there was a town around here called Rock Springs. He'd been through there once.

By nightfall he knew he had to talk to Tenawa and Standing Stone again. If they continued on the way they were going, without deviation, this ragtag group of reservation Indians was going to end up in Denver.

They camped as night fell, and Clint was able to slide from Duke's back without assistance. Once again, though, he sat on the side while the others did their part to build a camp for the night.

When Tenawa brought him his food he told her that he thought they were going to have to change direction.

"Why?"

"If we keep going west we're going to end up in Denver." When she looked blank, he added, "It's a big city with a lot of white people."

"Can we go north?"

"North, if I remember right, there's a town called Rock Springs."

"South, then."

"We'll come to another town sooner or later," he said, shaking his head. "No, I think we might have to put our plan into effect a lot sooner than we thought."

"You must tell Standing Stone."

"Yes. I will."

"And today, while riding, you thought of a plan?" she asked.

"I've got . . . something in mind, yes."

"That's good."

"Tenawa, you don't mind going back to the reservation?" he asked.

She gave him a stunned look.

"What's wrong?"

"You do not remember."

"Remember what?"

"You said you wanted to take me with you."

Had he said that?

"I think I said I'd *like* to take you with me," he said, "take you someplace safe."

"I thought . . ."

"You thought what?"

"Nothing," she said, and stood abruptly. "I will tell Standing Stone that you want to talk to him."

Before he could stop her she ran off, and he cursed himself for having hurt her feelings.

Winston Guest was disappointed that they had not caught up to the Comanches as soon as he'd hoped.

But they had caught up with them while there was still light.

"What now?" Henderson asked when they saw the Comanches.

"Let's withdraw a bit and talk it over," Guest said. "They ain't goin' nowhere."

They fell back a ways and dismounted to discuss their strategy.

"Nobody's riding back trail?" Henderson had asked, surprised.

"I wouldn't say that," Guest said.

"You saw somebody?" Elmer asked.

"No," Guest said, "but that don't mean they ain't out there."

"Wouldn't you see 'em if they was?" Elmer asked.

"I might be the best tracker of any white man alive, Will," Guest said, "but I still ain't no Indian. There could be somebody out there who just don't want to be seen."

"Then what do we do?"

"Let's just trail them until nightfall, when they'll camp."

"And then what?"

Guest thought a moment, then shrugged and said, "Damned if I know. I guess we'll just have to talk about it again. The important thing is that McLain and his trigger-happy troops aren't here."

"Well, if we wait too long," Henderson said, "they might be here."

"You're right," Guest said, "so we are gonna have to do somethin' tonight."

"Like what?" Elmer asked.

"Well, I guess I could ride on in to their camp and talk to them."

"That's crazy," Elmer said. "They'd kill you."

"You forget," Guest said, "these are reservation Indians. If McLain and his men went riding in there hell-bent for leather, somethin' would happen for sure. If I ride in alone I think I can talk to them."

"You know them, don't you?" Henderson asked.

"I know the old shaman, Standing Stone," Guest said,

"and I know a young hothead name of Bold Wolf. That's how I know that if McLain has his way the hotheads will prevail."

"Okay," Henderson said, "so we follow them until dark, and then you'll ride in and talk to the old man."

"Right."

They mounted up again and prepared to ride. Guest saw Henderson swiveling his head around in all directions.

"Forget it. I told you," he said, "if he don't want to be seen, he ain't gonna be."

"You said that," Henderson said, "but what I'm wonderin' is, could there be more than one of them out there?"

Guest didn't answer.

THIRTY-SEVEN

Spring had decided that they would take two hotel rooms.
Fall and Bunch would share one, while he would have his
own. That way he'd be able to take a whore back to his room.
He hated going to a whore's room or crib. You never knew
who was waiting for you there.

The whore he was with now was dark-haired, thin but with
big breasts. Spring liked his women to have big breasts. This
one was about twenty-five, so she wasn't worn-out yet, and
her breasts didn't sag yet.

"Ain't you tired of playin' with my titties, sweetie?" the
whore asked playfully.

He'd been fondling them and sucking on them for a good
half hour.

"How could a man get tired of playin' with a set of titties
like this, honey?" he asked.

He tweaked one of her brown nipples and she jumped.

"Don't it feel good?"

"It feels fine, sweetie," she said, even though he had just
hurt her. In fact, he'd been sucking on her and tweaking her

for so long that her nipples were starting to feel sore. She wondered if she was going to be sorry for agreeing to stay with him the whole night. At the time it had seemed better than being with five or six men for the same money, but now she wasn't so sure. At least the others would have been in and out of her real quick. This one wanted to take his time.

"Then I'll just keep on playin', if you don't mind," Spring said.

"Sure, honey," she said. "Play all you want."

"Tuck," he said, "my name's Tuck. Not sweetie, and not honey."

"Well . . . sorry. You called *me* honey, didn't you?" she asked.

"That's 'cause I don't give a good hard shit what your name is."

She was about to say something else, but he twisted one of her nipples again and then bit it and she tried not to cry out.

While he sucked on her nipples, he thought about what he and Bunch and Fall had talked about earlier in the evening . . .

Spring had met the others in a saloon for a beer after looking the town over.

"One lawman," Bunch said. It had been his job to find out if the town had a sheriff, and if the sheriff had a deputy. Bunch was good at talking to people, and Fall was not. What Fall was good at was arguing with people, so Spring had given him the job of finding the bank and looking it over.

"Just a sheriff and no deputy," Bunch said. "That's what people told me."

"You asked?" Fall said.

"No," Bunch said, "I just sort of let people tell me. People are real willin' to talk to a stranger in town."

"What did you find out, Ben?" Spring asked.

"They got a bank, all right, a little bitty one, but there's sure to be some money in it. Just while I watched I saw half a dozen people go in and out."

"And every bank's got a safe," Spring said.

"What do we do first, Tuck?" Bunch asked.

"First we get some fresh horses from that liveryman," Spring said.

"We gonna pay for them?"

"We're gonna take 'em," Spring said.

"What about the old man?"

"We'll tie him up, or kill him, if need be."

"What if somebody finds him?" Fall asked.

"Nobody's gonna find him, Ben," Spring said, "because we're gonna take the horses and hit the bank on the same day, and then ride out."

"They'll put a posse together," Fall said. "I hope what's in that bank is worth the risk."

"I don't know about you," Spring said, "but I'm tired of stealing from fellers like that one the bear killed. We never get nothin' but an extra rig, and some guns, and some clean shirts. It's time for us to graduate."

"Tuck," Bunch said, "you ever robbed a bank before?"

"No," Spring said, "you?"

"No."

They both looked at Fall.

"Don't look at me."

"How hard can it be?" Spring asked. "Just do what I tell you and we won't have a problem."

"What about the posse?" Fall asked.

"There won't be a posse."

"How do you know?"

"Because before we leave we'll kill the sheriff," Spring said, "and there won't be anyone to put a posse together."

"We're gonna be wanted in Colorado after this," Fall said.

"What's the difference?" Spring said. "They won't know our names. They'll just put some god-awful drawing on a poster that don't even look like us."

"You really think we can do this, Tuck?" Bunch asked.

"I know we can, Earl," Spring said. "Are you in?"

"I'm with you, Tuck," Bunch said.

"Ben?"

"I'm with you, Tuck," Fall said.

"Who kills the sheriff?"

Spring shrugged and said, "We'll draw straws."

"Turn over," Spring told the whore.

"Oh, honey—uh, Tuck, I don't like it that way."

"I do, and I'm payin'."

Great, she thought, turning over, not only were her tits going to be sore tomorrow, but her butt as well.

Spring got on his knees behind the girl, straddling her, and drove into her from behind. The bank job had him excited. Why hadn't he even thought of it before? With the money they took out of a bank he'd be able to afford better whores than this one.

He pumped in and out of her until he was good and wet from her, then withdrew, pressed the tip of his cock to her anus, and shoved. She gasped, reached out for the bedpost with both hands, and then moaned and groaned as he slammed into her until he emptied himself with a loud roar.

He withdrew and lay down next to her. She turned over onto her back, wincing.

"Gotta sleep," he said.

"Want me to go—" she started to ask, hopefully.

"No," he said, "stay. I'll just sleep for a while and then we'll do it again."

As he drifted off to sleep she decided that five or six quick in and outs for the same money would have been better than this, for sure.

THIRTY-EIGHT

When Bold Wolf came riding into camp, Clint knew that something was amiss. He dismounted swiftly and went to talk directly with Many Horses, Running Antelope, Little Buffalo, and the other young braves. He never once made a move to talk to Standing Stone, who was sitting with Clint.

They had just decided that Standing Stone would call a meeting tonight of all the men—old and young—and proclaim that Clint was, indeed, the Dreamwalker. After that it would be up to Clint to convince them to go back to the reservation by predicting disaster if they did not.

Clint and Standing Stone watched as the young men conversed intensely. Once or twice Bold Wolf looked over at them, disdain plain on his face.

"Looks like trouble," Clint said.

"I am afraid so."

"If they all try to ride out we're going to have to stop them," Clint said.

Standing Stone just looked at him.

"You don't think we'd be able to, do you?"

"Bold Wolf has a strong spirit," the old man said. "It ca
easily dominate others."

They watched and were surprised when the young men sim
ply dispersed and went back to their respective squaws c
camp fires.

Bold Wolf went to a fire, hunkered down, and began to ea
He no longer looked over at them.

"What was that about, I wonder?" Clint asked.

"I do not know."

"I think we'd better go ahead, Standing Stone," Clint saic
"Let's see how strong a spirit I have, and if I can dominate."

"How much do you know about the Dreamwalker?" th
old shaman asked.

"Some," Clint said. "Tenawa told me some things."

Standing Stone nodded. He did not seem surprised that hi
daughter had been helping Clint, teaching him.

"I hope she was a good teacher," he said, and stood up.

Clint watched the old man walk away and said, "So do I."

Tenawa came over to sit with him again while Standin
Stone tried to get everyone in place. The old men were easy
but it looked to Clint like the shaman had to do some seriou
talking to the young ones.

"Tenawa, about before—" Clint started, but she cut hir
off.

"It does not matter. I should go back to the reservatio
That is where I belong."

"That's not it," he said. "I—I am not a man who stays i
one place very long. I travel a lot."

"You do not want me for your squaw," she said. "I un
derstand this."

"No, I don't think you do. You see, I don't want *anyon*
as a squaw. I am not ready to be married."

She looked at him.

"It is not just me that you don't want?"

"No," he said. "I'm not ready to give myself to anyone i
that way, yet. That is what I want you to understand."

"Then perhaps . . . someday?"

What should he say to that? he wondered.

"Who knows, Tenawa?" he asked. "Who can tell the future?"

She smiled at him then and surprised him by saying, "The Dreamwalker."

Clint grinned back, then looked over to where Standing Stone and Bold Wolf were talking, nose to nose.

It did not look good.

THIRTY-NINE

Standing Stone and Bold Wolf separated. The shaman walked back over to where Clint was sitting with Tenawa. The headstrong young brave melted into the shadows.

"What happened?" Clint asked.

"The others will sit and listen," Standing Stone said.

"Not Bold Wolf?"

"He did not say yes, and he did not say no."

"Did you find out what he was talking to the others about?"

"He would not say."

"All right, then," Clint said. "Where do you want me?"

"First I must make a wheel."

Clint knew he meant a Medicine Wheel.

"When that is done, we will sit and you will talk."

Clint nodded and said, "All right, Standing Stone. Just tell me when and where you want me."

The old man nodded, then looked at his daughter, who immediately stood up and began looking for stones for the Medicine Wheel.

• • •

"What are they doin'?" Henderson asked.

He, Guest, and Elmer were watching the camp from high atop some rocks, far enough away to go undetected—they hoped—but close enough to see what was going on.

"They're making a Medicine Wheel," Guest said. "This is a ceremony few white men get to see, fellas."

"Have you seen it?" Henderson asked.

"Once," Guest said, "when I was very young."

"Why are they doin' it now?" Elmer asked. "Are they lookin' for some kind of magic to help them get away?"

"No," Guest said, "somethin' else is goin' on."

"Like what?"

"Wait . . . okay, look there. See?"

Both Henderson and Elmer strained their eyes to see what he meant, and then saw it.

"That's a white man," Henderson said, surprised.

"What the hell is he doin' there?" Elmer asked.

"Right now," Guest said, "it looks like he's gonna sit in on a Medicine Wheel ceremony."

"Is that unusual?" Henderson asked.

"It's unheard of," Guest said, shaking his head.

"Then what's he doin' there?" Elmer asked.

"That's an interestin' question."

Clint sat as part of the circle the Comanches had formed, but all eyes were on him as if he were at its center. What was at its center, however, was the Medicine Wheel.

"The circle is never ending," Standing Stone said, "life without end."

Before Standing Stone could speak of Clint and the Dreamwalker he had to smudge everyone present. Smudging was the use of smoke to clear away negative energies and to attract positive energies.

Clint watched with interest as Standing Stone walked to each person, holding a wooden bowl from which smoke was coming. He first brought the smoke toward his heart, and then held it over his head. That done he offered the bowl to the four directions, to Father Sky and to Mother Earth. He then pushed his thumb into the bowl until it was covered with ash and then smudged each person's forehead with it.

When he set the bowl down, Clint thought he was finished, but Standing Stone picked up a pipe and proceeded to light it. The bowl of the pipe was made of stone, the stem of wood, and the pipe was covered with feathers. While the shaman was putting tobacco into the bowl he offered a pinch to the four elements, the spirit kingdom, Mother Earth, Father Sky, Grandmother Moon, and the Great Spirit. (Clint didn't know any of this at the time, but it was explained to him by Tenawa later on.)

Standing Stone lit the pipe and offered a puff of smoke in each of these directions. He then passed the pipe on and every other person in the circle did the same thing. When it came to Clint he had watched it so many times he knew what to do.

That done, Standing Stone walked to Clint and pointed down at him.

"This man," he went on, pointing to Clint, "is the Dreamwalker."

FORTY

There was a sharp, collective intake of breath, and even though all eyes were on him to begin with, Clint suddenly felt pressure, as if their eyes were actually touching him.

"How do we know this?" one of the elders asked.

Standing Stone looked surprised and said, "I am telling you."

"We need proof," the man said, and others nodded and murmured their assent.

Clint spoke then, loudly, clearly, and with more confidence than he felt.

"Would you have me do magic tricks?"

Everyone fell silent.

"Fly through the air?" He looked directly at the questioning elder. "Make *you* fly through the air?"

The elder leaned back, actually looking frightened.

Clint pursed his lips and emitted a short whistle which no one understood until they saw Duke—the "Black Stallion"—come trotting over. Several men scrambled out of the way, breaking the circle so Duke could enter it. Once inside Duke faced Clint, completely still except for his quivering muscles.

Clint stood up, went to Duke, and touched his muzzle.

"I challenge anyone here who does not believe in me to come here and touch the muzzle of the Black Stallion. If I am lying, nothing will happen . . . if I *am* the Dreamwalker, he will bite off your hand."

Clint knew that he was taking a big chance, but he had to convince these people quickly. The only one he thought might challenge him was Bold Wolf, but he was not present. In fact, Clint hoped to get this all over with before the young brave returned.

He stood at Duke's head, turning and looking at each of the people in the circle. He looked longer at the young braves, like Many Horses, Running Antelope, Little Buffalo, and they each in turn looked away.

"It is accepted," Standing Stone said. "What would you have us do, oh great Dreamwalker?"

"Go back."

"Go back . . . where?" Many Horses asked.

Clint turned and looked directly at the brave who had spoken. Many Horses wanted to look away, but something would not let him.

"Back to the reservation."

"What?" Many Horses said.

"We can't!" Little Buffalo said.

"How can we?" Running Antelope asked.

There were more questions coming from the others in the circle, and Clint waited for them to die down before speaking again.

"If you stay out here, you will all die," Clint said. "The soldiers will come."

"We will fight them," Many Horses said.

"That is why you will die," Clint said, "because you will fight."

"Are you saying we should not fight?" Running Antelope asked.

"That is exactly what I am saying," Clint replied.

Running Antelope stood up abruptly.

"Bold Wolf was right!" he snapped. He did not bother to say what Bold Wolf was right about, but stalked away from the circle.

Many Horses stood up after a moment, and then walked the same way as Running Antelope.

Little Buffalo then stood up, said, "I will not go back," and followed the other two.

Three other young braves also stood and left, but the rest stayed.

"Will you go back with us?" one of the elders asked.

"No," Clint said, "I cannot. I have . . . uh, other things to . . . to do. Standing Stone will take you back safely. He is your shaman. You will obey him as you would the great Dreamwalker."

Clint fell silent then and, with Duke in tow, left the circle. He breathed a sigh of relief. It could have been worse. More than six people could have resisted him. Maybe Standing Stone would be able to talk to the six young men who left and persuade them.

Tenawa came over to where Clint was standing with Duke.

"Standing Stone says we will turn back tomorrow," she said.

"You'll probably meet soldiers along the way. You can give yourselves up to them, but it will be important not to make any threatening moves."

"Standing Stone knows that."

"Good."

"What will you do now?" she asked.

"I'll stay here," Clint said, patting Duke's neck. "I'll rest up, heal, and then move on."

"To where?"

"I don't know, Tenawa," Clint said. "Well, actually, I do."

"Where?"

"I'm going to find the three white men who robbed me while I was injured. They have my saddle, my saddlebags, my guns, and my clean shirt."

"Clean shirt?"

"That was a joke," he said. "I really want my guns back, though."

"And you want to kill them."

He didn't answer. Did he want to kill them? As he saw it, what they had done to him was almost as bad as shooting him in the back. They had come upon him helpless and hurt and instead of helping him, they had robbed him and left him to die. If the Comanches had not come upon him, he would be dead now.

He knew he wanted them to know that he wasn't, but beyond that he didn't really know what he wanted to do.

"I should stay with you," she said. "You will need care."

"I'll be fine, Tenawa," he said. "You and your father have done all the work, already. Now the only thing left for me to do is heal. You belong with your people."

"Back on the reservation."

"Wherever they go."

She was going to say more but was interrupted when Standing Stone came over.

"How did they take it?"

"I think many of them are relieved," Standing Stone said.

"And the six who walked away?"

"They are still in camp. I will talk to them."

"And Bold Wolf?"

"I do not know where he is, but I do not think he will go back."

"He'll be alone," Clint said. "If a few of the others stay with him, they're only going to get themselves killed."

"They are young men," Standing Stone said. "They would rather die than go back to the reservation."

"Maybe you can talk them out of it."

"I do not think so."

"Why not?"

"If I was a young man," Standing Stone said, very seriously, "I would be going with them."

FORTY-ONE

"What was that all about?" Henderson asked.

He, Elmer, and Guest had slipped to what they hoped was a place far enough away from the Indian camp, where they had made a cold camp.

"I'm not sure," Guest said. "It was a Medicine Wheel ceremony, but I don't know what the white man and then the horse were doing there."

"That was some horse, wasn't it?" Elmer commented.

"Yeah, it was," Guest said thoughtfully. "You don't see many horses like that . . ."

"What are you thinking?" Henderson asked.

Guest didn't respond immediately, and when he did he just said, "Nothin' important."

"So what do we do now?" Elmer asked.

"We take turns standing watch and wait until morning," Guest said. "That's when I'll go in and talk to Standing Stone."

"You think you can convince him to come back with us?" Henderson asked.

"I hope I can," Guest said. "When McLain and the others catch up to us, I want to have the situation well in hand."

From a place above the three white men, Bold Wolf looked down on them. Why had the Army only sent three men after them? Or maybe these men had just been sent ahead to scout. Now that they had found the People, Bold Wolf wondered what they were waiting for. While they had watched the Medicine Wheel ceremony, Bold Wolf had watched them. When the three men made their way back to their cold camp, Bold Wolf had followed them. Now it looked as if they were going to go to sleep for the night, with one man on watch.

Bold Wolf could not do anything alone, not tonight. He had seen Many Horses and the others walk away from the Medicine Wheel, so he knew that they were not happy about whatever Standing Stone and the white man had said. He decided to go back to camp and talk to them. The seven of them could ride back here in the morning and kill the three white men. That way when the rest of the soldiers found them, they would know that the Comanches—these Comanches—were not just reservation Indians anymore.

They were warriors.

"What should we do?" Many Horses asked.

Bold Wolf had slipped back into camp unnoticed and was now talking with Many Horses, Running Antelope, Little Buffalo, and the other young braves who had walked away from the ceremony.

"We do what true warriors would do," Bold Wolf said. "We show the Army that true warriors will not live on reservation."

"How do we do that?" Many Horses asked.

"In the morning we will ride to the white men's camp and kill them all. That will send a message to the white soldiers."

"At last," Running Antelope said, rubbing his hands together, "we get to fight someone."

While the others agreed it was about time, Many Horses was not that sure.

Clint lay down on his blanket and hoped that when daylight came these people would not change their minds. He wondered what the six braves who walked away were going to do, and then he wondered about Bold Wolf. If the headstrong young brave convinced the other six braves to ride with him, the seven of them could wreak a lot of havoc in the area for a while, until they were hunted down and killed.

Clint decided there wasn't that much he could do about it. If the young men in the camp didn't want to listen to him, what could he do? Especially after Standing Stone himself said he would be riding with them if he was their age.

Clint had almost drifted off to sleep when he was aware of someone approaching him. He opened his eyes and saw Tenawa creeping toward him slowly.

"Tenawa, what are you doing?"

"Here," she said, thrusting a gun and holster into his hands.

"Where did you get this?"

"It is Bold Wolf's."

"He'll miss it."

"It is a trophy for him," she said. "He does not use it. He does not know how. You will need it tomorrow."

Before he could thank her, she went off as quietly as she had come. Clint checked the gun, saw that it could use a cleaning but that it was in working order. It was an old cavalry Colt, probably once belonged to some soldier. He wondered how Bold Wolf had come to have it.

He lay back down with the gun next to him. He hadn't realized how naked he felt without a gun until now. Then he wondered what Tenawa had meant when she said he'd need it tomorrow. Was it because the Comanches would be going back and he'd be staying behind? Or was there another reason? One that had to do with Bold Wolf?

FORTY-TWO

When Clint woke the next morning it was with a sense of foreboding. He sat up and looked around, saw that the Comanches were preparing themselves to travel again. As he got to his feet he saw Tenawa moving toward him.

"What's wrong?" she asked when she saw his face. "I was about to wake you."

"Where is Standing Stone?"

"He is over—"

"Did Bold Wolf come back?"

"I have not seen him."

"And the others? Many Horses, Running Antelope, the others who walked away from the Medicine Wheel last night?"

"I saw Many Horses," she said. "I do not remember seeing—"

"Run and check for me, Tenawa, please," Clint said. "Go and see if you can find the others."

Confused, she said, "A-all right . . ."

As she hurried away Clint turned, picked up the gun she'd brought him the night before, and strapped it on. It wasn't his, but it certainly felt more comfortable than *not* having a gun on.

Tenawa came running back.

"They're gone," she said. "They're not in camp, and their horses are gone also."

"Where's Many Horses?"

"He is here."

This confused Clint.

"Why didn't he go with them?" he wondered out loud. "He walked away when they did."

"Do you want me to ask him?"

"No," Clint said. "Find me Standing Stone. Your father and I will ask him."

Bold Wolf was gone, and five other braves. Many Horses was not with them, but Clint felt sure that he would know where they went.

When Standing Stone came over, Clint explained his fear, then they went to talk to Many Horses.

When the young brave saw them coming his way, he looked around nervously.

"Many Horses!" Standing Stone said. The tone of his voice froze the young man. "Where are Bold Wolf and the others?"

"I . . . I do not know."

"I think you do know, Many Horses," Clint said. "They must have left early this morning, and you were smart enough not to go with them. Why?"

"I—I—"

"Many Horses," Standing Stone said sternly, "you must tell the truth."

"They—they have gone to kill the white men."

"What white men?" Clint asked.

"The ones Bold Wolf saw following us."

"How many?" Clint asked.

"Three."

"Soldiers?"

"Two soldiers," Many Horses said, "and one who is not."

Two soldiers and probably a civilian scout, Clint thought.

"Bold Wolf must have spotted them, but he didn't move on them until he had help." Clint looked at Standing Stone and said, "They have to be stopped." He asked Many Horses, "When did they leave?"

"At first light."

Virtually minutes ago.

"Get your horse," he said to Many Horses.

"Why?"

"Do you know where they went?"

"Bold Wolf told us where the camp was—"

"You're going to take me there."

"I should go with you—" Standing Stone said.

"There's no time, Standing Stone. Come later if you wish, with the others, but Many Horses and I have to go now." He looked at the young brave. "Are there enough rifles for Bold Wolf and the others to be armed?"

"Yes."

"Get your horse!"

The first bullet struck Corporal Will Elmer in the right thigh, waking him up.

Winston Guest dropped the coffeepot and cup he'd been holding and rolled over behind his saddle for cover as a volley of shots followed that first one. At the same time he yelled for Henderson and Elmer to wake up. He didn't know at that moment that Elmer had been hit.

Henderson woke up, tangled in his blanket, and reached for his rifle. As he did so something tugged at his right sleeve. He took cover behind his saddle and checked his arm. The bullet had gone through his sleeve and left him with a scratch.

Will Elmer was not so lucky. He had to drag his wounded leg to get behind the cover of his saddle.

"Anybody hit?" Guest asked, after the shooting had stopped.

"I am!" Elmer shouted back.

"Bad?"

"Right thigh," Elmer said. "It's not so bad."

"Tie it off tight, Will. Stop the bleeding."

"Yeah, yeah," Elmer said, tying his bandanna around his thigh as best he could, "tell them to quit shootin' at us."

"Henderson?"

"I'm okay."

"Anybody see anything?"

"Hell no!" Henderson said. "We were asleep, you were on watch."

Guest didn't have to be told that. He *knew* that, and he was angry with himself. By all rights the first bullet should have struck him, not Elmer.

"We're lucky Indians are lousy shots with a rifle," Henderson called out.

"Yeah," Elmer said, "lucky."

They could tell from Elmer's voice that he was in pain. Pinned down like this, neither one of them was going to be able to help him. Guest probably could have made his way over there, but even if he made it without being wounded they wouldn't be able to share the cover of Elmer's saddle.

"What do we do, Guest?" Henderson called.

"Let's see if they'll talk," Guest suggested. Louder, he called, "Hey, in the rocks!"

The reply was a volley of shots, fired almost halfheartedly.

"Guess they don't want to talk," Henderson said. "Now what?"

"Well," Guest said, "judging by that volley I count at least three or four, maybe more."

"If there were many more," Henderson reasoned, "they'd probably just come riding down here."

"That's true," Guest said, "so let's call it half a dozen. We're outnumbered. . . . ." He listened a moment, then called out, "Elmer, you still with us?"

"I'm with ya," Elmer called back.

Guest nodded and said, "We're outnumbered two to one."

FORTY-THREE

Clint heard a volley of shots and realized they weren't that far away. He was following Many Horses and he realized that he might be riding into a trap. What if Bold Wolf left Many Horses behind specifically to lead him into it? He couldn't afford to think that way now. There were three white men out there, probably pinned down. If the Comanches killed them, there'd be no going back for any of their people.

There was another, shorter volley of shots and Clint wished that Many Horses's pony could go faster.

Bold Wolf realized that he and the others were too far away. That they had hit even one of the men was pure luck. They were just not very accurate with rifles, which felt foreign in their hands.

"We must get closer," he called out.

"I will go first," Running Antelope volunteered.

He stood up and started down the hill toward the camp, screaming at the top of his lungs. One of the white men stood up, shouldered his rifle, and fired once. Running Antelope stopped screaming and fell to the ground, rolling the rest of the way down the hill.

Bold Wolf watched as Running Antelope stopped rolling. He did not get up, but he could see that the man was still breathing.

"We must all rush them at one time," he called out to the others.

"They have cover," Little Buffalo called out, "and we will have none."

"Do you think your fathers and your grandfathers worried about that?" Bold Wolf called back. "On my word we will rush them . . . or are you cowards?"

Bold Wolf heard a sound from behind, the scrape of a boot on rock.

"On *my* word you will throw down your weapons."

Bold Wolf turned his head and saw Clint Adams standing just above him, holding a gun. *His* gun.

The other braves were looking at Clint, too, and behind him Many Horses, holding a rifle.

"Many Horses, shoot this white man," Bold Wolf said.

Clint was relieved to hear Many Horses say, "I cannot, Bold Wolf."

"We can kill him easily," Bold Wolf told the others. "We are five to one. Many Horses will not shoot him, but he will not shoot us, either." Bold Wolf looked at Clint with disdain and said, "He is not the Dreamwalker."

"I don't have to be," Clint said, cocking the hammer of the gun and pointing it directly at Bold Wolf's head, "to kill you."

Winston Guest saw the lone brave start down the rocks toward the camp.

"Stay down!" he called out to the two soldiers. He then stood, calmly raised his rifle, and fired one shot. Guest was an excellent marksman, which the Indian brave discovered the hard way.

He ducked back down behind his saddle and waited for what was to come next.

"Hello the camp!"

It was a white man's voice. Was it a trick? No, there had been a white man in the camp. At the time Guest had not been able to tell if he was there willingly or not. He guessed that they were about to find out.

"Who's up there?"

"My name is Clint Adams," the voice called. "I'm coming down with the Comanches. Hold your fire."

"What do we do?" Henderson asked.

"Clint Adams," Guest said. "I thought the man in camp looked familiar. He's the Gunsmith."

"The Gunsmith!" Henderson said, in surprise.

Guest called out loudly, "Come ahead!"

He, Henderson, and Elmer gaped at the scene of one white man holding a pistol and one Comanche with a rifle walking five other Comanches—unarmed—down from the rocks.

"Check Running Antelope," Clint said to Many Horses.

Clint marched Bold Wolf and the other four into the camp. From behind Many Horses called, "He is alive."

"Everybody all right here?" Clint asked.

"We've got a man hit," Guest said. He turned and looked at Henderson, who was checking Elmer's wound.

"He'll live," the sergeant said.

"That's good," Clint said, "that's very good. Nobody was killed."

"Yet," Guest said. "Mr. Adams, do you mind if I ask what you're doing with these runaway Comanches?"

"That'll take some time, Mr. . . . "

"Guest, Winston Guest."

Clint looked Guest up and down.

"I've heard of you, Mr. Guest."

"And I have heard of you, Mr. Adams."

"Is it just the three of you?" Clint asked.

"So far."

"How much time do we have to talk?"

"Not much, I'd think," Guest said, "so I guess you better talk fast."

FORTY-FOUR

When Lieutenant Kenneth McLain saw the renegade Comanches ahead of him, he held up his hand and stopped his troop's progress.

"Private Thomas!"

With Henderson and Elmer gone, McLain had named Private Jim Thomas his second.

"Yes, sir."

"Get the men ready."

"Sir?"

"We'll charge them," McLain said, and Thomas's eyes grew wider as he saw the lieutenant draw his saber. "I will lead the charge."

"Uh, sir?"

"Yes, Private?"

"I see Mr. Guest and Sergeant Henderson with them, sir."

"What?" McLain looked again and saw that his private was right. Not only were Guest and Henderson with them, but Corporal Elmer as well.

"That's fine," he said. "We'll put them under arrest as well."

"Sir?" Thomas asked, shocked. "Arrest our own men?"

"You heard me, Private Thomas."

Thomas just sat his horse and stared at the lieutenant.

"Sir, those Indians are not armed. I, uh, I think they've surrendered to Mr. Guest and Ser—"

"Private Thomas," Lt. McLain said, turning his head and glaring at the man, "are you questioning my orders?"

"Sir," Thomas said, "riders approaching."

McLain brought his head around and saw Guest, Henderson, and Elmer approaching with two other riders, one white man and the other the Comanche shaman, Standing Stone.

"What's this?" he said, unaware that he'd said it out loud.

"Lieutenant," Winston Guest said, "put that saber down."

Clint was impressed with Winston Guest. He thoroughly confused the young lieutenant by insisting that he had cleared it with the officer to take Sergeant Henderson and Corporal Elmer with him to find the Comanches.

"I gave no such permission," McLain said.

"If you think back, Lieutenant, I think you'll recall that you did," Guest said, and then hurried on. "Imagine our surprise when we found them and they surrendered to us."

"Surrendered?" the officer asked.

"Yes, sir. They're ready to go—well, almost all of them are ready and willing. A few of them are going against their will, but they're going."

He was speaking of Bold Wolf and his braves, who were—for the moment—tied up until Standing Stone could talk some sense into them. Clint felt that by the time they reached the reservation, Bold Wolf might be the only one still tied up.

"It's all over, Lieutenant," Guest said. "We can go home."

"Now wait just a minute—"

"I am honored to surrender to a great warrior," Standing Stone said to McLain.

The lieutenant stared at him, and then asked Guest, "Who's he talking about?"

"Why you, Lieutenant," Guest said. "Who else?"

FORTY-FIVE

After the Comanches and the soldiers started back to the reservation—Lt. McLain still somewhat confused, but apparently mollified by Standing Stone's deference to him—Clint decided not to stay camped where he was, but to ride to Rock Springs. His back had taken the hard ride on Duke well, and the town was only about two hours to the north. A couple of days in a bed—and a visit to a doctor—would do wonders for him.

The hardest part was saying good-bye to Tenawa. He knew he had disappointed her by not asking her to stay with him, but he just couldn't do it. For one thing, she would have taken it as a proposal of marriage, and he definitely was not looking for a wife.

Bold Wolf still regarded Clint with hatred, especially since he'd made him back down in front of his men. Clint thought the Comanche brave should have been born twenty years sooner. He would have been a great warrior.

By the time Rock Springs appeared ahead, Clint was ready for a real meal, a real bed, and a beer.

He got a lot more than he bargained for.

• • •

Tucker Spring was finally ready to hit the bank.

Bunch and Fall were starting to think they were never going to rob this bank.

"Conditions have to be perfect," Spring insisted.

Spring went back and forth between the bank and the saloon, checking conditions, until he was finally satisfied.

"The sheriff's in his office," Spring said. "We hit there first, and then the bank. Got it?"

"We got it," Bunch said.

"We've had it for hours," Fall said.

"Don't smart off at me, Fall," Spring said. "You're gonna thank me for this when we've got money in our pockets."

"Then let's go get it."

They left the saloon and walked across to the sheriff's office. Spring had decided not to kill the man. A shot would be heard, and none of them were adept at killing a man close up with a knife. Instead, they entered the office, got the drop on him, tied and gagged him, and locked the lawman in one of his own cells.

"Okay," Spring said, "let's go hit that bank."

Clint rode into Rock Springs and realized that, for a while—lying helpless after the bear attack, and even in the Comanche camp—he'd thought a time or two that he might never see a real town again. Rock Springs was by no means a large town, but it had everything a town should have. It had a saloon, and a feed store, and a hardware store, a hotel, a bank . . . and at the moment three men were coming out of the bank carrying sacks. It did not look as if they had just made a legal withdrawal, not the way they were backing out with their guns drawn.

Clint jerked on Duke's reins and directed the gelding over toward the bank. The men did not see him until they turned to get on their horses.

"Hey, fellas . . ." he called.

They looked at him and everything happened quickly after that. There was no law around that he could see, and these men had obviously robbed the bank. Still, if they hadn't had their guns drawn things might have been different.

One of the men made the fatal move, starting to point his gun at Clint.

"Don't!" Clint shouted, but now it seemed they were all bringing their guns around.

Bystanders later said he drew and fired three times before anyone knew what was happening.

Two of the bank robbers staggered back, shot in the chest. The bags of money fell to the ground, spilling some of the bills onto the dirt.

The third man actually got a foot in the stirrup of his saddle. Clint's bullet struck him in the shoulder and, left foot in the stirrup, he tried to fire back. Clint shook his head slightly to himself and fired again. The bullet went through the man's left side, damaging both his heart and his lungs. He fell backward onto the ground, his left foot twisted in the stirrup.

Clint dropped down from Duke's back and grabbed the horse before it could run off, dragging the man down the street. He disentangled the man's foot from the stirrup as people came running out of the bank.

"They just robbed the bank!" a young man shouted. He was wearing a white shirt, a bow tie, and suspenders. "Where's the sheriff? They just robbed the bank!"

An older man in a suit approached Clint and said, "You just stopped a bank robbery, mister."

"I was just riding in," Clint said.

"Lucky for us," the man said. "My name's Zollinger. I'm the bank manager. Are they dead?"

Clint looked at the three men. Two were dead, but the third, though mortally wounded, seemed to still be alive—though not for long.

"Wait a minute—" Clint said.

"What is it?" the manager asked.

"This man looks familiar to me."

He leaned over the wounded man and looked down at him. The last time he'd seen him had been at a similar angle, only the man had been leaning over him.

"These three men robbed me a couple of weeks ago."

The man on the ground looked up at him, his eyes glazed.

"Remember me, friend?" Clint asked. "You and your friends found me lying on the ground after a bear attacked me. You stole everything I had."

"You—" the man said, recognizing him. "You're dead."

"No, I'm not," Clint said, as the man died, "but you are."

Clint searched the man and found his New Line Colt in his belt. He hoped he'd find his other belongings as easily.

"Lucky coincidence, huh?" bank manager Zollinger asked.

Clint, who normally hated coincidences, said, "Yes . . . this time."